A Hope Springs Novella

My Dearest

A HOPE SPRINGS NOVELLA

MY DEAREST

SARAH M. EDEN

Interior design by Heather Justesen
Edited by Annette Lyon and Lisa Shepherd

Cover design by Mirror Press, LLC, and Rachael Anderson
Cover Image © Giovan D'Achille / Trevillion Images

Published by Mirror Press, LLC

ISBN-10: 1-947152-07-6
ISBN-13: 978-1-947152-07-6

Chapter One

New York, Autumn 1860

Ian O'Connor spent his days in the corridors of purgatory itself. The thick air rang with the aggressive crash of machinery and the unending din of voices. The factory offered the poor an income but precious little else. Within the dark confines of their daily prison, they worked and collected their pay with no expectation of joy. Yet on an autumn day, as he walked the length of a nearly windowless stretch of hallway, Ian crossed paths with an angel.

He saw her for only a moment, a chance encounter. He'd finished maintenance on a parawind ring spinner with only moments to spare before the arrival of the first shift of workers. More machines had needed attention, and he'd rushed down the corridor to see to them. A group of workers passed him going the other direction, chatting and interacting. His gaze caught on one woman in particular, keeping a bit apart from the others, her gaze on nothing in particular, her thoughts apparently wandering. She passed a narrow window, and the fiber-filled light illuminated her face. Something in her expression—a mixture of uncertainty and determination—tugged at him.

That moment replayed in his thoughts again and again long after he'd returned home to the cramped tenement his large family called home. The unnamed woman had simply walked past. She hadn't spoken, hadn't even looked at him. Yet the moment had seized hold of his mind and heart.

It had been but an instant that passed as swiftly as a summer's breeze. The memory, rather than settling in his mind as it ought, had wrapped itself around his very heart, expanding in his chest in a way somehow both painful and pleasant.

Into his whirl of thoughts came his da's voice, half-laughing, half-scolding. "If you go on as you are, Ian, you'll leave far and plenty enough food for even Patrick here."

That pulled him fully into the moment. Those of his family who worked the earlier shift, as he did, were gathered for the early evening meal. They all watched him, laughter in their eyes. Little Finbarr grinned, his gap-toothed grin in full evidence, though he likely didn't actually know why the situation was funny, he being only five years old.

Ian didn't intend to lay his thoughts bare for all of them. A man had to be allowed some secrets, even when sharing a tiny flat with six people. "We could all of us skip this meal, and there'd still not be enough to satisfy Patrick. The lad eats as though he has a hole in his stomach."

"I am sitting right here, you looby," Patrick said between generous spoonfuls of soup.

2

"He's seventeen years old," Da continued as though Patrick hadn't spoken. "You ate every bit as much at his age. And thank the heavens we had the means of feeding you. You'd've gone hungry back in Ireland, if you'd survived at all."

His family seldom spoke of home or the Hunger that had driven them to this foreign place. The reminder hit Ian like icy water.

"I'd not meant to sound ungrateful." He dropped his eyes even as he dropped his voice.

"I'd not thought you had," Da answered. "Eat, though. You're needing your strength. The overseer's not abiding any slowdowns."

Ian knew it well enough. They worked themselves to exhaustion each day, but no amount of effort ever seemed enough for the demanding Mr. Hunt. The entire family, excepting the oldest brother, who drove freight, and Ma, who cleaned houses, made their living within the walls of that miserable place.

Still, Da had gained some favor with the factory owner, a man with greater sway than the overseer, if not as much direct influence over their daily experience. Mr. Grandford's approval helped make the family's situation more stable than most, and more secure than they could find elsewhere. Enduring the unpleasant overseer was worth those benefits.

"What is it that has you so distracted?" Patrick kept his voice low so only the two of them were likely to hear.

Only Tavish, who sat in age between the two, came close to matching Patrick in talkativeness and willingness to give a fellow a hard time if ever the opportunity arose.

"'Tis no thing, truly," Ian said. "I'm a bit weary, is all."

Patrick only eyed him more pointedly over his own bowl of hot soup. "We're always weary, you and I, leaving for work as we do in the wee hours each morning." He motioned with his chin to Ian's neglected bowl of soup. "This picking at your food is something new."

There would be no escaping Patrick's curiosity once they retired to their shared sleeping space. Patrick would have all the night long to hound Ian until he was forced to confess simply to get a bit of rest. Truth be told, of anyone in his family, Patrick was the most likely one Ian would confess to. Though five years separated them, they were thick as thieves. From the time Patrick was born, they'd spent every day of their lives together. Ian trusted Patrick more than anyone else. He possessed a wisdom that went beyond his seventeen years and a cheery personality that couldn't help but lift one's spirits no matter how heavy.

Ian kept his voice low as well. "Have you ever seen something so unexpected, so . . . perfect . . ." That wasn't the right word either. "I don't know how to say this. You know I haven't the gift of gab like you and Tavish do."

Patrick's gaze darted to their parents, both distracted by Finbarr's telling of a dramatic story about a bird. The lad had, on account of his time spent amongst the children of the families Ma worked for, formed a manner of speaking equal parts Irish and American.

"Allow me to use m' talents to interpret what you're fumbling over." Patrick's eyes had a way of dancing about when he was holding back a laugh. "I believe what you're trying to tell

4

me is that today you crossed paths with a woman, one who likely didn't so much as notice you. And she, in that bit of a moment, claimed your heart and soul."

How in heaven's name had Patrick sorted that much from Ian's fumbling, incomplete explanation? "That's—a bit frightening."

Patrick nodded slowly and with emphasis. "Seems I inherited Granny O'Connor's second sight. Or"—he backed away dramatically from his bowl, eyes wide with feigned amazement—"perhaps the fact that you and I work alongside each other all the day long may mean I witnessed the moment you nearly walked into a wall because you'd locked your gaze so firmly on a certain lass with nut-brown hair. It's one of those two possibilities, I'd wager."

Finbarr's story yet held Ma and Da's attention. Ian bent over his bowl, but continued his conversation with Patrick. "She was an angel, I'm full sure of it."

"Does this angel have a name?"

"I'd imagine she does."

Patrick chuckled low. "You didn't at any point during the day manage to learn her name?"

Ian held his hands up in frustration. "I never saw her again." He'd raised his voice without meaning to, so his declaration caught Ma and Da's attention. Da looked curious, but Ma looked downright captivated.

"Saw *her*?" she pressed.

"Her?" Finbarr repeated, his little voice matching Ma's tone precisely. The lad then burst into laughter. He was a happy child.

At the moment, though, that happiness felt a little too close to mockery, no matter that the boy was only a wee thing.

"I'm for bed," Ian said, standing. "Morning'll come sooner than it ought." He crossed to the quilt hanging from a rope on the far side of the room, behind which he and Patrick had their small corner.

"But, Ian," Ma called after him. "You were speaking of a woman."

He turned back. "Not I. 'Twas Patrick."

"Patrick!" Ma's voice rang with eagerness.

Patrick shot him a look of promised retribution. Ian only grinned and slipped behind the quilt, into the relative privacy it offered. He had full faith in his brother's willingness to keep Ma off the scent for a time.

He lowered himself to the folded blankets that were his bed and leaned his back against the wall, his legs bent in front of him. He hadn't the slightest idea who his angel was, what her name was, or where she lived. He couldn't even say with certainty in which part of the factory she worked.

He knew only one thing with surety: somehow he would find her again.

Biddy Dillon had known her share of misery. Stepping out of the gates of the textile factory long after dark, surrounded by her fellow Irishmen, she knew her experiences were not entirely unique. They'd all suffered these past years. Suffered and struggled. Wept and worried. And somehow, through it all, they'd managed to survive. She had every intention of continuing to do so.

But on days like this one, that goal seemed ever harder to reach. The overseer, a great, lumbering man with thick whiskers and sharp eyes, had loudly berated her, standing so close as he'd shouted that he could easily have struck her if he'd chosen to. The encounter had left her shaken. Not only was he, himself, a frightening figure, but this factory had a reputation for firing workers for the slightest misstep. She desperately needed the work.

Biddy was alone in the world, with no one to turn to should life grow even more difficult. Her meager earnings barely stretched between paydays. She had a survival plan: toe the line and get her work done without making the least bit of trouble. 'Twas something of a joyless way of living, but it'd seen her through a great many difficulties.

A few of the girls she worked near waved to her as they turned down their street. Another small group did the same at the next corner. She had the farthest to go, and night after night, she made the last half of her journey alone.

Two other workers stepped alongside her. She had seen them each night making their way home. She suspected they were brother and sister; they bore a noticeable resemblance to each other.

The girl, likely no more than fourteen or fifteen, turned her head toward Biddy and spoke. "Mr. Hunt ought not to have done what he did today. I'm sorry for it."

The siblings were Irish. She might have guessed as much. Most of the factory workers shared her homeland.

The brother turned a worried countenance in Biddy's direction. "He didn't hit you, did he?"

Biddy shook her head but couldn't manage an explanation beyond that. Those worrisome moments in the factory still hung too heavy on her heart for conversation. 'Twas a terrible thing to be at the mercy of a tyrant.

"He railed at her for long minutes over broken threads," the girl explained to the boy. "We've all had them break at one time or another. The whole lot of us were quaking where we stood."

The brother nodded slowly, with understanding. "Likely what he wanted to happen."

Once again the girl's gaze was on Biddy, filled to brimming with empathy. "Why must he be so brutal?"

"Personally," her brother jumped in, "I believe it's the whiskers."

He made the unexpected pronouncement with such solemnity that Biddy couldn't stop herself from turning toward him and staring a bit. His gaze shifted in her direction for just a moment, long enough for her to see a teasing glint in his eyes.

"His whiskers?" She was appreciative enough for the change in tone that she happily encouraged it.

The lad nodded solemnly. "I am convinced within myself that his whiskers itch terribly. 'Tis such a torture that he can't help but be a miserable lout all the day long."

A lightness Biddy seldom experienced wrapped itself around her heart. "That must be it."

"I am Ciara, by the way," the girl said. "And this is my brother Tavish."

Biddy nodded her acknowledgment. "I'm Biddy."

"We'll see if we can't kidnap a barber to bring with us tomorrow," Tavish said. "Perhaps Mr. Hunt will show himself to be a sweet soul once his face is clean shaven."

Biddy knew that wasn't the case. She felt certain that these two siblings knew it as well. Still, they'd helped lift a burden on her heart, and she was grateful for it.

"Perhaps we'll see you tomorrow," Ciara said.

"I hope so."

The brother and sister turned down a side street. She truly regretted their departure despite having only just made their acquaintance. She liked them. Their open manner and optimism, especially in the face of difficult circumstances, spoke to a need deep in her heart. Long years had passed since she'd felt the hopefulness they exuded. She wanted to believe that life could be lived, not merely survived. Too many harsh experiences had taught her otherwise.

Keep your mind in the moment, Biddy.

She walked the dark, quiet streets. The path, though familiar, did not allow for wandering thoughts. She kept an eye on every shadowy corner, turned to check anything that moved. Her boarding house sat at a far distance from the factory, but 'twas all she could afford. Life had given her few choices.

Her mother's oft-repeated words echoed in her thoughts. We make the best of it. Come what may, we make the best of it.

Biddy told herself as much again and again every day, as she covered the distance to the boarding house and as she jostled for room in the cramped and tiny kitchen, attempting to make herself something to eat.

And she told it to herself again ever more fervently as she lay awake on a tiny cot in a cold corner of the room she shared with six other women. Above her head, she heard the same couple raging at each other as they did every night. She heard the cries of babies penetrating the thin walls around them. She felt the creeping chill of approaching winter, a reminder that her small blanket would soon prove insufficient.

Make the best of this life. This wearying, difficult life.

Chapter Two

No matter how difficult the task of staying awake during a long and drawn-out mass, Ian could always count on Patrick and Tavish to wake him up on the walk home. This week, however, they managed the thing by teasing him ceaselessly about his fruitless search for the still unidentified woman from the factory.

But his time at work was not his own. He hadn't the leisure to wander in and out of the various rooms, searching faces for the one more angelic than the heavens themselves. He felt certain she arrived at the factory with the main influx of workers, a full two hours after he began his work day, and, as such, left hours after he did as well. Their time in those cold and impersonal walls overlapped in the cruelest way, with their precious few moments of freedom coming too far apart for another chance meeting.

"Have you thought, Ian, that maybe you only imagined this mythical woman of yours?" Patrick had quite the talent for managing an entirely serious tone when he was anything but. "Seems maybe your wits have at last gone begging."

They wove around a crowd of people on the street.

"You saw her your own self," Ian said. "You told me so."

Patrick shook his head, his lips turned down in a look of great sadness. "Now you're imagining conversations. This cannot be a good thing." He turned to Tavish. "Should I break the news to Ma about Ian's mind turning to mush, or do you mean to?"

"It'd be best coming from me." Tavish nodded solemnly. "She likes me better than either of you."

"The two of you aren't nearly as funny as you think you are."

Patrick's brow drew low. "I am almost certain that is not true."

"As you said," Tavish jumped in once more, "the man's wits have gone begging. He no longer knows what he's saying."

"You're fair askin' to have your nose broken, now aren't you?" Ian gave his brother a light shove.

Tavish dodged the intended blow, barely managing to not bump into any of their fellow pedestrians. "I'd not want you to overtax yourself, old man."

Patrick chuckled low and deep. "You *are* growing a bit decrepit in your old age."

Ian took a teasing swing at Patrick, who stumbled backward, pretending to have been felled by the unlanded punch. Tavish jumped into the fray with more laughter than fire. The crowded streets afforded little room for horseplay, yet Ian and his brothers managed it nearly every Sunday. They pushed and slugged and generally let out the energy that had built inside them while sitting so long on an uncomfortable bench, listening to a priest—and that after six days spent in endless repetition of tasks and movements in the factory.

"Enough." After one particularly well-placed elbow sent Tavish tumbling into the teeming street, Ma's voice cut through the din of the city, the people mulling about, and her sons tossing insults at each other. "Don't you lads make me curse on the Sabbath."

"Sorry, Ma," they all three muttered in unison.

"If you were truly sorry, you'd not be fighting those grins in your eyes I see clear as day." She shot them a look every Irish mother perfected the moment her first was born. 'Twas a warning, and the laying of guilt, and the promise of eternal punishment should her children further transgress. Yet it also included an unmistakable amusement and love tucked in there somewhere. "Set a good example for Finbarr, won't you?"

Their youngest brother walked alongside Ma, his bright, eager eyes taking in every inch of the city and the countless people they passed. Say what one might of New York, it offered an endless stream of sights and sounds.

Ma hadn't finished her lecture. "He'll have far enough difficulty determining the kind of lad he ought to be, growing up as he is in this den of villainy, without his own brothers proving themselves a collection of hooligans." This was the point in Ma's scolding when she usually swatted them and allowed her fondness to show in her eyes. Not this time. "Be the men I raised you to be, or, I swear on the saints, I'll box your ears, Sabbath or no Sabbath."

The three of them exchanged surprised looks. Had they truly upset her? Ian hoped not.

Tavish moved immediately to Ma's side, offering quiet, sincere apologies and attempting to soothe her ruffled feathers.

"He never can abide anyone in the family being unhappy," Patrick said, watching their brother's attentions to Ma.

"She does seem unhappy, doesn't she?" Ian didn't like seeing it any more than Tavish did. What had brought this heaviness on, though? Ma was generally in good spirits.

Patrick spotted one of his friends—he had a great many—and hurried off toward him. Ian was not, however, left on his own long. Da stepped up next to him.

"Did you spot your angel in church, by chance?" Da asked.

Ian offered a half-hearted smile. The entire family had taken to teasing him about his fruitless search, even his two oldest siblings, Grady and Mary. Though they both were married and living in flats of their own, they'd come by with the sole intention of giving him a thorough pestering.

"No, I didn't find her. It seems fate is playing a cruel game with me."

"Ah, bad luck, that." Da's gaze drifted ahead of them to Ma walking with Finbarr's hand firmly in hers. "Did your ma give you a tongue lashing?"

"She did." Ian stuffed his hands into the pockets of his outer coat, protecting them from the cold. "Is all well with her? I've not known her to be so short with us over a bit of pushing and pulling."

Weariness settled heavy on Da's face. "She's not happy here.

14

'Tisn't at all the life we once knew, these closed spaces and neighbors so near you hear them through the walls, yet so distant you're not sure of their names."

"She misses home." Ian missed Ireland as well, though he'd lived there only fourteen years before they'd left. Ma had called it home for far longer.

"That she does. But 'tis more than that. She misses the quiet and the long moments of peace." A soft sigh slipped from Da's lungs. "This entire country is pressing and pulling at itself, threatening to shatter into bits. The tension and anger hovering over the land worries her fiercely, especially knowing that her children's futures are tied to this nation's."

Ian had heard a few of the whisperings, so he knew what Da referred to. "The election must not be too far off now."

"Only a couple of weeks, and I'm troubled, I am."

They nodded to a few people as they passed by. Even on a late Sunday morning, the streets of New York weren't quiet or still.

"Is it a particular candidate you're worried over?" Ian asked.

Da shook his head. "'Tisn't the men running but the ones voting that have me nervous. I've heard tell of terrible things that happened this past year, and there's a lot of talk about horrible things to come if this man or that man isn't chosen as president."

Ian had heard many the same rumblings. Portions of the country threatened to break away if the candidate they most supported wasn't victorious. Though the O'Connors had been in this country only a few years, he understood the end result of such a thing: armed conflict.

"How is it we've the misfortune to have left behind one nation torn to bits by starvation, only to land in another about to destroy itself by war?"

Da shrugged, the gesture one of forced lightness. "I've long suspected one of our ancestors crossed a particularly vengeful fairy."

"I'm believing that more and more all the time."

Da's smile turned easier, more natural. "You'll find your mysterious woman, son. I'm full certain of it. The fates can't be that cruel."

He wanted to believe it, but fate had, indeed, been terribly cruel any number of times.

"That brother of yours, though," Da continued, "he can't seem to rid himself of the lasses. Every time I turn around, Tavish is smiling at another girl or two."

"Or three or four," Ian added.

The sound of Da's laughter did Ian a world of good. The haunted look that had filled the countenances of so many during the Hunger never fully left his parents' faces. He wished he could give them the open spaces and peace they longed for. None of them were finding those things in New York; that was for certain.

Except for Patrick, truth be told. For reasons none of them could sort, he was very nearly thriving. He'd found a set of friends, managed a bit of socializing on Sundays when he wasn't working. He didn't enjoy his job, but he seemed to be enjoying his life.

Ian's gaze fell not on Patrick, who had disappeared with his friends, but on Tavish, who walked down the street with a lass on either side of him. How he managed to catch their eyes so quickly and effortlessly, Ian would never know. Likely in part because he was handsome as sin. Patrick would likely be the same in another year or two.

The lass on Tavish's right turned a bit toward her companion, bringing her into profile. He knew her in an instant. Recognized her.

Good heavens.

"You look as though you've seen a ghost," Da said.

Ian shook his head, not taking his eyes off the woman he'd been searching for. "Not a ghost. An angel."

"You've found her, then? Where?"

"Where else?" He motioned ahead of them. "With Tavish."

Da gave him a nudge. "A bit of effort, and she'll be talking with *you*."

The idea sent his heart thudding, but his mind would have none of it. "I've not Tavish's gift for conversation. After him, she'll find me terribly dull. They're likely closer in age anyway."

"Tavish is not much younger than you are," Da said. "Even if the lass is nearer him in age, that's not such a terrible thing. Your ma and I have six years between us."

Ian didn't know whether to laugh or protest. "I think you've jumped far ahead of things, there, Da."

"If you don't make a go of it, there'll be nothing to jump ahead of." Da nudged him once more, a bit more firmly this time.

Ian allowed himself to be hurried in the direction of the nameless stranger. A few people stood between them, necessitating a bit of weaving about on Ian's part. His heart picked up pace as he drew closer. The sound of it in his ears nearly drowned out everything else. A moment more, and he was at Tavish's other side, his brother having been abandoned by one of his female companions, though, thankfully, not the one Ian found most important.

"Well, good day to you there." Tavish greeted him with a laughing grin.

Ian opened his mouth to reply, but nothing emerged beyond the vague sound of choking. That set *her* gaze on him. He only choked more.

Tavish's brows angled low as he eyed Ian sidelong. Ian swallowed against a lump of embarrassment in his throat and let his gaze drop to the walk ahead of them.

"Oh." Tavish's whisper held an alarming amount of dawning realization.

How Ian hoped his brother wouldn't humiliate him. One could never be fully certain with a nineteen-year-old who possessed a penchant for humor and teasing. Had Patrick been there, the two of them would've launched into full-fledged taunting without hesitation.

"Biddy, this is m' brother Ian," Tavish said. "Ian, this is Biddy Dillon."

Biddy Dillon. He knew her name at last.

Ian looked over at her once more, intending to offer an actual greeting. She was smiling at him, her blue eyes lit with what looked like genuine pleasure at meeting him, a sight that set his mind to mush.

"A pleasure to meet you, Ian O'Connor." His angel was Irish. "I've seen you at the factory."

She'd seen him? And she'd noticed him enough to remember? The shock only tied his tongue into greater knots. All he could manage was a nod.

An awkward silence hung in the air as they walked on. Tavish, still between them, gave Ian a series of frustrated, laughing, pointed looks. He even tossed in a few subtle nods in Biddy's direction.

The man had a point. He'd been looking for Biddy—heavens, it was nice to have a name for her—these past days, even losing some hope of finding her. Now she was here. He couldn't simply go on without saying anything. But what?

"Biddy!" a woman's voice called through the small crowd around them. "Biddy!" The new arrival ran up directly to Biddy's side and took her arm. "You'd best hurry. Mrs. Garrety is in a rare taking. She's insisting the Macafees haven't paid their rent."

"But they have," Biddy said. "I was there when they did."

Her friend nodded anxiously. "That's why we need you. She's threatened to send for the police and have them tossed out. Everyone who saw them pay means to stand up for them."

Quick as that, Biddy left, hurrying off to help her friends. Ian watched her go, as disappointed by her departure as he was impressed by her reason for going. Not a moment's hesitation had delayed her rush to another's aid.

"You, Ian O'Connor, are something of a dunderhead." Leave it to a younger brother to ruin a moment of rare, soul-deep hope.

"How do you figure that?" Ian asked.

Tavish shook his head, lips pressed together in amused annoyance. "You've been beside yourself thinking you'd never find that chance-met angel. Then here she was, but you didn't say a word to her."

Had he really not spoken to her at all? No. He must've managed to say something. Hadn't he?

"She likely thinks you hardly noticed her," Tavish said. "'Tis a full shame, is what it is."

As the older brother, Ian hated to admit when Tavish was right. But there was no denying it this time. Fool that he was, Ian had let uncertainty get the best of him. He'd made a mull of the entire thing.

Chapter Three

Seldom did the crushing sound of the large spinning machines grow silent in the textile factory. Only ever at night, when the workers were gone or when something broke, making the machines grind to a halt.

Though grateful for a momentary reprieve from the deafening sound of the machines after half a day of enduring the noise, Biddy stood still and worried, watching the overseer pace the length of her row of spindles. Whatever had gone wrong had happened near her station. She'd not done anything differently from what she always did, so she couldn't possibly be at fault. That fact, however, would likely not prevent her from being blamed.

More than one section of spinning machines had been stopped, as they were all connected to one another. Her fellow workers stood about, chatting and gossiping as they were wont to do when given a rare moment for socializing. Normally, she might have joined them, but Mr. Hunt's look of displeasure warned her not to seem to be enjoying the break even the least bit.

He looked past her. "There you are. Took you long enough, O'Connor."

O'Connor? Tavish and Ciara's surname. Two of their brothers tended to the machines; Biddy had seen them both around the factory, fixing and repairing things.

"What's happened?" the newly arrived O'Connor asked.

Biddy didn't look over at the sound of the quiet, calm voice. She felt more at ease at the simple sound of it.

"The machine's stopped," Mr. Hunt grumbled. "You're supposed to inspect them each morning. What are we paying you for if you don't keep them running?"

Biddy snatched a glance at Ian—she remembered the name from when Tavish had introduced them on Sunday. Ian hadn't seemed overly interested in making her acquaintance, but he'd not been unkind, either.

Just now he wore a look of unruffled patience directed at Mr. Hunt. Biddy envied him the ability to remain calm under the glare of the too-often violent overseer.

"I did, indeed, inspect these machines this morning before any workers arrived. Before *you* arrived, in fact, though you're supposed to be here when inspections begin." He raised a single ginger brow. "Perhaps Mr. Grandford would care to know that you aren't entirely certain that the machines are properly looked after because you don't arrive when you're meant to. An owner would likely be very interested in such goings on in his factory."

The overseer turned a shade of angry red that went from the top of his long forehead all the way to the bottom of each jowl.

Ian didn't seem the least worried. He stepped to the end of Biddy's row, where he disengaged the wheel that connected that section of spinning machines to the wheels overhead that powered them.

"Did the trouble with the machine begin in this section, then?" he asked Mr. Hunt.

"Yes, here on Biddy's line." Mr. Hunt jammed his thumb in her direction. "Likely wasn't paying enough attention."

Now 'twas Biddy's turn to redden. She didn't dare argue on her own behalf. Mr. Hunt already thought the worst of her.

Ian looked at her then, the first time since his arrival. His gaze lingered but proved unreadable. Was he pleased to see her? Surprised? Did he even remember her? The moment ended as quickly as it had begun, and his attention turned to the machines.

"Did you hear any odd sounds before the movement stopped?" Ian asked her.

"I did," she said quietly. "A bit of a squealing and then grinding."

"You *were* paying attention, it would seem."

The overseer's mouth drew down sharply at the subtle contradiction of his earlier claim.

Ian walked along her line of spindles slowly, eying them carefully. He stood so close by, but he didn't look at her again. Odd, that. But, then, mechanics occupied a place of importance above the spinners. Some of them took that clout entirely to heart.

"Did the sound seem to come from above your head or down here, near the floor?" he asked.

"Down here. Among the spindles."

He simply nodded, continuing his slow perusal. Ian could not have been more than a few years older than she was, same as many of the other young men in the factory. Yet he seemed older than the others. Not in a bent or worn-down way. Rather, he was calm and sensible, not prone to fits of temper or overly eager to show himself to be happy or in a good humor. He seemed comfortable with who and where he was. In Biddy's limited experience, that was a rare trait indeed. 'Twas a calming and reassuring thing, as well.

Ian stopped his movement down the line and bent closer, studying the many lines of thread and various sizes of spindles.

"Found something?" Mr. Hunt asked, moving to hover nearby, looking over Ian's shoulder.

"I did." He set down his box of tools, selecting a pair of sheers from among them.

"The problem *was* in this section, then." The overseer spoke to Ian but glared at Biddy.

"The problem"—Ian leaned over the spindles, the sheers in his hand—"is that you employ only two pickers for this entire section." He snipped a set of threads. After switching his sheers for a pinching tool, he reached into the narrow gap down toward the gears.

"I don't see what the pickers have to do with this." Mr. Hunt couldn't seem to decide which of the two of them—Biddy or Ian—he was most irritated with. His narrowed gaze jumped between them. "If she broke her equipment—"

"There's a thick buildup of cotton waste between two gears." Ian turned a bit, clearly struggling to reach it. Large arms weren't meant to fit in such a small space. Though he'd stopped the machine, any number of sharp parts and tiny spaces could pinch and cut him.

"Do be careful." Biddy couldn't keep the concern from her tone.

"Hush, woman," Mr. Hunt barked.

Ian met her eye. Somehow he smiled without the tiniest movement of his mouth. Warmth began to replace the cold grip of worry deep in her chest.

"Hire the pickers you're meant to have," Ian said, "and you'll see fewer moments when bits of cotton and fluff floating about clog up the machines."

With sudden but careful movements, he pulled his arm free. A thick and blackened bit of cotton lay in the grip of his pinching tool. He held it up for Mr. Hunt to see. "A small thing, but it'll do a fair bit of damage."

Ian tucked the blackened cotton into the pocket of his leather apron. He reengaged the mechanizing wheel, and the spinning machines groaned as they resumed their movement, almost as if they were as wearied by their daily interactions as the workers themselves.

"Back to your jobs," Mr. Hunt shouted at them all, quite as if long hours had passed since the machinery resumed operations rather than the few minutes that had gone by.

Ian dropped his tool back in his box.

"Thank you," Biddy said.

Would he know she meant the words as more than gratitude for fixing the machine? He'd defended her against Mr. Hunt's accusations. He'd spoken on her behalf. She'd not had a champion of any kind since before her mother died. She remembered too little of her father to know if he'd ever filled that role. A woman alone in the world needed a friend now and then to keep her from losing all hope.

Ian dipped his head in response to her expression of gratitude. "You're quite welcome, Miss Dillon."

Miss Dillon. She liked the sound of her name spoken in his calm and soothing voice. She'd very much have liked to hear it again, perhaps even a more personal version of her name. That would require some degree of closeness between them. Friendship, at the very least.

She felt herself blush ever deeper at the sudden turn of thought. A man, admittedly a handsome and kind man, had shown her a bit of attention—not enough for anyone to take notice—yet her mind had jumped to longing for a more personal connection to him.

"Get moving, Biddy," Mr. Hunt barked. "You have broken threads to tend to."

Those words held more wisdom than he could possibly have known. Every thread in her life, it seemed, was broken. Standing about wishing otherwise wouldn't fix any of them. What she needed was to move, to work, and to find new threads, new connections.

She was ready to stop being so entirely alone.

Chapter Four

Nearly every Sunday evening, all the O'Connor children gathered together. Though the small tenement was crowded with twelve people tucked inside, their moments together were joyous. Ian sat on the floor not far from the stove, watching his family talk and laugh.

"Oh, how I long for the open spaces of home," Ma bemoaned to Mary. "We'd not be so cramped when we gather if we still had so much room."

'Twas as Da had said a couple of Sundays earlier: Ma was unhappy in the close confines of the city. But the family had no options, no means of escape.

Grady, the oldest, sat not far off, talking with Da. The tenement was larger than some claimed by other families. Still, no conversation was ever private. Without any effort, Ian overheard their discussion as well as he'd heard Ma and Mary's.

"I can't see any outcome that'll not lead to something worse than the state of things now," Grady said. "Every delivery I make, someone is speaking of the election, of the tensions with the South, and the possibility of war."

"It worries a soul, it does." Da shook his head slowly with clear regret and more than a drop of concern. "Despite our miseries here, this country saved us from starvation. I'd hate to see America tear itself apart."

The look of pale worry on Ma's face told Ian that he wasn't the only one who'd overheard the heavy discussion. He wanted to set her mind at ease, but what could he say that wouldn't be either insufficient or a lie?

Every possible outcome of the swift-approaching election would result in greater troubles. The country was too divided, too angry, too ready to fracture.

Ian met Tavish's eye, silently asking his brother to summon his usual heart-lightening charm. Tavish didn't wait even a moment.

"Now, Ma, you'll never guess who it was I saw walking home from church this morning, looking fresh as a morning daisy. And, because I know you'll never guess, I'll give you an enormous hint."

Ma had turned her attention to him. Ian only hoped Tavish's story would be enough of a distraction.

"My hint," Tavish continued. He wiggled his eyebrows and widened his eyes. "She's a young lady, somewhere near my age. Quiet, but not overly so. Sweet natured. Works at the factory." His eyes darted to Ian but returned almost instantly to Ma. "She's been described by a certain older brother of mine as 'an angel.'"

Ah, saints. Leave it to his troublemaking brother to choose *this* topic as a distraction.

Tavish now had everyone's attention. How was it that Ian's interest in Biddy had become a topic of fascination for the entire family?

"Did she ask about Ian?" Ma didn't seem to think that an unlikely possibility, though he knew better.

"I didn't speak to her." Tavish sighed with deep drama. "Ciara did, though."

All eyes were now on the younger of the O'Connor sisters. She only laughed. Ian shot Tavish a look of promised retribution. This bit of humiliation would not go unanswered.

"Did she ask after Ian?" Ma pressed her hands together as if praying for an affirmative answer.

Ian felt half tempted to pray for a miracle of his own: a means of distracting his family from this ill-conceived distraction. "I can't imagine Miss Dillon would even remember me, let alone ask after me," he said. "I've only spoken with her once, and it wasn't anything memorable."

Except that he'd been something of an idiot, rambling on about machines rather than managing to speak of anything personal or interesting.

"I'm certain she remembers you, Ian," Ma insisted. "How could she not remember such a lovely man as yourself?"

"Quite easily, Ma. Quite easily."

Her expression turned stern. "Do not count your value so cheaply, son."

Patrick joined in, which all but guaranteed the conversation would turn anything but serious. "She has a valid point, Ian.

You're quite the catch, you know, though you are ginger. You've that aura of mystery about you. The lasses can't resist that."

Tavish never needed an invitation to join in a bit of joviality. "Indeed. I'd wager every single woman in this entire city is clamoring for any bit of your notice. Crying themselves to sleep, they are, poor girls."

Ian never could be fully put-out with his brothers when they picked at him this way. Indeed, he was too grateful at seeing the light return to Ma's eyes to be the least bit annoyed that he was the brunt of their harassing.

Little Finbarr, who'd been standing beside Grady, crossed to Ian. He assumed a look of utmost pity, then spoke in words too stilted to have been anything but memorized. "You shouldn't make the lasses so miserable. It isn't sporting of you."

Ian looked quickly at Grady and saw a grin so mischievous as to tell him that all of his brothers were now bent on taunting him over his inept attempts to capture Biddy Dillon's notice.

Finbarr pressed his hands over his mouth even as a laugh jumped out of him.

"You think this is so funny, do you?" Ian grabbed at Finbarr and pulled him into a one-armed hug, using his free hand to tickle the lad under his ribs.

"Stop, Ian!" Finbarr giggled through his half-hearted objection.

"Why? Is it not *sporting* of me?"

Finbarr wriggled in his arm, twisting enough to free a hand and make his own attempt at tickling his much larger, much older brother. Though the lad's tiny fingers had no real impact,

Ian pretended to be equally tortured. The little giggles were well worth the required playacting.

Not more than a minute into their good-natured scuffle, the sound of ripping fabric brought everything to a halt. Ian followed Finbarr's horrified gaze all the way to the gaping hole in his own left sleeve.

"I'm sorry," Finbarr whispered. "I didn't mean to break it."

Ian ruffled the boy's shockingly red hair. "All'll be well, lad. Don't fret over it." His hair had once been that same color but had calmed and eased over the years into a shade closer to sand than to carrots.

"But this is your working shirt," Finbarr said. "What'll you wear to the factory tomorrow?" His brow drew in further with every word. "What if you're fired?"

"Fired?" Tavish tossed out. "Why, without a shirt, he'd be the most popular man in the whole place. The spinning room alone would work extra fast for the promise of a brief glimpse of his muscles."

"And a certain Miss Dillon would likely fall to pieces at the sight of him," Patrick added. "That'd be well worth the draftiness, don't you think?"

Ian shot them the driest look he could manage. It didn't help. They only went on joking.

Ma, between laughs, told Ian to change back into his finer Sunday shirt so she could mend his work shirt before morning.

He paused long enough to give Finbarr some reassurance, then stepped behind the quilt hanging over his and Patrick's corner of the tenement. He pulled off his shirt, and dropped it on his blanket, then reached for his Sunday shirt on its unusual nail in the wall. Except the shirt wasn't there. He didn't see it on the floor. It hadn't managed to get tucked under his blanket.

Where could it have gone? He pulled up both his and Patrick's blankets. He checked the small trunk they kept their other things in. The shirt was nowhere. He had only two to his name. Despite working in a cloth-making factory, they couldn't afford more than two shirts apiece. Losing one would cause no end of trouble for the family's finances.

He'd simply have to keep searching. The shirt had to be somewhere.

He pushed back the quilt, intending to comb every inch of the place if need be. Everyone turned, staring at him wide-eyed. His eyes, however, settled on only one person. A newly arrived, unexpected addition to their gathering.

Biddy Dillon. Sitting amongst his family. And there he stood, without a shirt on.

Ian didn't know who started laughing first, but he'd have wagered it was Patrick. In an instant, all the room was roaring with it. How did he manage to make a fool of himself every time he saw her?

He hurriedly ducked behind the quilt. He could still hear them laughing. If he waited there long enough, she'd have time to leave so she wouldn't have to face him—and he wouldn't face her.

Why can't I manage even one moment with her that shows me to advantage? Just one.

The quilt moved. Ian braced himself. No matter who came

through, the situation would only grow worse. The women in the family would come offering pity, which would add to his embarrassment. The men would come with every intention of mocking him, which he was not at all in the mood for.

"Ma had already put our Sunday shirts in the basket for laundering tomorrow." Patrick had stepped into the space behind the quilt. For once he didn't sound on the verge of laughing.

"I looked like an idiot," Ian muttered.

"I'd wager she didn't think so."

That idea was ridiculous. Ian couldn't help but turn and glare at his brother. "I was parading around half-naked. I'm surprised she didn't stand up and walk out on the instant."

"She didn't stand up or walk out at all, brother." Patrick held out a wad that Ian suspected was his Sunday shirt. "She's sitting with Ma, waiting."

"Waiting?"

"For you, you lummox. Now, take the shirt and go face her like a man."

He snatched the shirt but didn't move to put it on. Though being cowardly wasn't his preferred style, he found himself unequal to the moment.

"Pull yourself together, Ian." Patrick set a hand firmly on his shoulder, keeping his voice low. The flat was a small one, and a quilt hardly prevented conversations from being overheard if undertaken at anything over a whisper. "She seems a sweet-hearted lass. And if she's not been frightened off by our enormous family or the sight of your bare chest"—he smirked the tiniest bit as he mentioned that part of this mess—"then I'd say she's well worth the awkwardness of facing her just now."

He was right, of course. Ian flicked out the shirt and pulled it over his head. "Thank you for the encouragement." He spoke as quietly as Patrick.

His brother shrugged. "Someday when I've met a girl of m'own, you can talk me around to having the needed courage."

"You're seventeen. It might be a few years yet." Still, Ian smiled. "When the time comes, I'll offer all the advice you could possibly want."

"I'll hold you to that no matter how many years pass." Patrick tugged on Ian's arm, now covered in a shirt as it ought to be, then shoved him back around the side of the quilt.

The family had managed to get their laughter under control, though their eyes still danced with merriment. Biddy was, as Patrick said, still there. She didn't look at him with disgust, or revulsion, or pity, or any of the other things he'd imagined. She truly looked pleased to see him.

"You've a visitor, Ian." Ma didn't bother hiding her giddiness.

He offered what he hoped was a calm and welcoming smile in Biddy's direction. "Good evening to you, Miss Dillon."

She rose and crossed toward him, stepping around Finbarr and Ciara, who were seated in the middle of the room. Ian forced each breath past his nervous lungs. He couldn't quite swallow. His head filled with the sound of his own heartbeat.

"I hadn't meant to interrupt," she said once she'd reached his side. "I—" She looked back over her shoulder at the family, who were, of course, all staring.

Over her head, Ian shot them all a look promising retribution if they made this any more uncomfortable than it was. Quick as lightning in a storm, they took up conversations with one another, their gazes diverted.

Biddy looked at him once more. "I only wanted to thank you," she said, her voice lowered. "I never had the chance to tell you that I appreciate your standing up for me when Mr. Hunt tried to blame me for the machine breaking."

It hadn't been such a heroic thing as she made it out to be. "I couldn't stand there listening to him blame you when you'd done nothing."

Her expression brightened a bit. Heavens, he loved her smile. "I can think of a great many other men who'd've done just that."

"And I can think of a great many women who'd not've bothered to offer their thanks."

A bit of color touched her cheeks. "That was all I came for," she said. "I'll not disrupt your family's evening further."

His lingering embarrassment over parading about with his shirt off was immediately overpowered by panic. He never saw her. Not ever. Their time at the factory overlapped, but their leisure moments didn't. He had a rare chance for her company, for an opportunity to get to know her, but she was leaving.

"You could—you could stay."

She shook her head. "I couldn't."

Ma answered first. "Of course you could. It'd be grand to have you."

"I can't." She spoke softly, her hands clutched in front of her and her brow pulled in something very like concern.

35

"You'd be no imposition." Ma grew more insistent. "We'd love for you to stay, wouldn't we?"

The family answered with enough enthusiasm to frighten off even the stoutest of hearts.

To Biddy's credit, she didn't flee nor melt into a puddle. "I thank you for the invitation. Truly, I cannot accept. I've only a small window of time every few days when I'm granted use of the stove. I need to return to fix my meals for the next while. I truly *cannot* stay."

Ian nodded his understanding. Disappointment prevented him from speaking actual words. Her departure wasn't a rejection. She wasn't leaving because she disliked his company. At least, he hoped that wasn't part of her reasoning.

He stayed rooted to the spot as Biddy navigated back to the door, the family wishing her farewell as she went. *Say something, you dunderhead.*

He quickly formulated a farewell of his own, one not too personal, but not too uninteresting, either. He took a breath, ready for when she turned back for her final goodbye at the door.

But she didn't. She opened the door and walked out without so much as a glance back. Had she not regretted leaving even a little? Had she not wanted one last look?

How is it I manage to make a mess of every encounter with her?

Chapter Five

Biddy's walk to the boarding house on Monday night proved more pleasant than usual. Her time with the O'Connors the day before buoyed her spirits. They had been kind and welcoming. Ian—she pushed back a smile at the thought of him— was the one who invited her to stay.

When he first retreated behind the quilt at having been caught only half-dressed, she thought he might not come back out. But he had. And he'd spoken with her. She didn't know him well, but what she knew, she liked.

The fond memories very nearly pushed away thoughts of Mr. Hunt. Today, like most days, he'd growled and grumbled; at times, he shouted and raged. Always at her, and always without reason. Through it all, she worked as hard as she knew how, hoping to prove herself productive enough that he'd not fire her. She didn't love the work. She very nearly hated it. But without money, she'd lose her place at the boarding house. She'd lose the only roof she had over her head, her only haven from the unforgiving world. She had to keep her employment no matter how miserable it made her.

She pulled her coat more firmly around her as she continued the long walk along the dark streets. Winter had not yet arrived, but the night air had a bite.

We make the best of it, she silently repeated her mother's words. Come what may, we make the best of it.

Heaven knew she was trying, but there seemed so little for her to cling to. If only they'd not left Ireland. If only they'd not left her father.

She didn't often allow herself to explore those long-hidden memories, but at times like this, when she was overwhelmed and tired and sad, they simply flooded over her.

She'd been only six years old when they left. The Hunger had been in its earliest years then, yet it had already fiercely clutched their corner of Ireland. All around them, neighbors, friends, and even strangers walked about with empty eyes and empty bellies. She was old enough then that she ought to have remembered more than she did, but whenever she allowed herself to think on those times, the memories were vague and incomplete.

The most specific of them was a tall, stone building that was intimidating, frightening. She and her mother went there many times toward the end of their days in Ireland. They stood in front of it, gazing up at its thick grey walls, but Biddy didn't know why. After their arrival in America, she'd asked her mother about the building a few times, but the answer had always been the same: "We'll not think on those days, Biddy. It doesn't do to dwell on pain."

Biddy had no recollection of her father being with them

during their trips to the worrisome buildings. Mother had insisted that he hadn't abandoned them, but he wasn't in any of Biddy's last memories of their homeland. Mother had also insisted that he meant to join them in New York. For years, she'd sworn that he would yet come. But she'd died alone, and now Biddy was all that remained of her family.

A hard, bitter wind brought her attention back to the dark streets. She ought to have been more attentive. While she'd have liked to believe she wasn't in danger, she was of too practical a bent to ignore the possibility.

She'd gone far enough that only the O'Connor siblings were still walking the same path. They'd be turning off at the next corner. Biddy would do well to be more alert after that. She'd be entirely on her own for the last stretch.

When they reached the corner, someone stood there. A man. The gas lamp nearby didn't illuminate him quite well enough to identify him or make out any distinct features. Her heart beat harder, nervousness making her tense and unsure. What if this stranger decided to follow her?

"Ian?" Tavish called.

The shadowy figure stepped closer. It *was* Ian. Far from settling into a state of calm and ease at the realization, Biddy's heart kept pounding, but pleasantly this time. She managed a smile when she was about to pass him. He returned the gesture, but didn't follow his brother and sister around the corner. Rather, he walked beside *her*.

"I hope I'm not overstepping myself," he said, "but Ciara told me last night that you make a good portion of this walk alone."

"I do." The family spoke of her in private? She didn't know whether to feel uncomfortable or flattered.

"Merciful heavens, Miss Dillon. 'Tis full dark out, and this isn't a safe city."

She knew that well enough. "What choice do I have? I cannot afford any of the boarding houses closer to the factory, and I must both have a job and a place to lay my head." 'Twas a short but crucial list, one heavy on necessity and horribly light on joy. "It is what it is."

He shook his head and continued walking alongside her. "My mind'll be more at ease if you'll allow me to walk with you, to see to it that you arrive safely home."

The unexpected declaration stopped her in her tracks. "Why would you do that for me? We hardly know each other."

He stuffed his hands into his coat pockets and kept his gaze firmly ahead. "Perhaps I'm simply a good-hearted fellow."

"'Twould be reassuring to know there is at least one in this world," she muttered.

That brought his gaze to her. The night was too dark for seeing his expression, though she'd guess it held confusion, perhaps a bit of disapproval. She'd admitted more than she'd intended. This time she was the one to look away.

"Is the overseer shouting at you again?" he asked quietly.

Her heart dropped anew. "I don't know why he took such an instant dislike to me. Perhaps he can sense how desperately I need the job and sees me as a chance to lord over someone." The cold air nipped her face. "I'm trying to imagine spending the rest of my life fighting to hold on to a position I dislike so much."

She began walking again. When he didn't immediately follow, but hesitated, watching her, she motioned for him to join her. He quickly did so.

"If you could do any job in all the world, what would you pick?" he asked.

Thank the stars for the lighter topic. Thinking on her actual future always depressed her spirits. Speaking in *what ifs* was far more pleasant. "I would like almost anything that would take me away from the noise of the city. A house somewhere, with enough land for a large garden. I miss having earth about, a place to work the soil and grow things."

"You were a country lass in Ireland, I'd wager."

"I was," she said. "But I was very young when we left, and I've lived here far longer than I lived there. It doesn't make sense to feel more at home in those memories."

"The Irish countryside gets in one's veins, Miss Dillon. The passage of years can't change that."

She looked up at him as they walked, side by side. "Were you from the countryside as well, then?" He understood the pull too well for anything else to be true of him.

He nodded. "I was."

"And do you miss it?"

"With every fiber of myself. I'm grateful for a job that keeps my family fed and housed, but heaven knows I'd far rather have earth beneath my feet than these cobblestones, to have land stretching all around me instead of crowded streets. 'Twould be a dream come true, that would."

How was it she was having such a personal conversation

with a man she hardly knew? And how was it that his company didn't make her uncomfortable? She generally kept to herself.

"This is where I live," she said, motioning to the rundown boarding house.

He eyed it, clearly unimpressed. Who would be? There was a reason she couldn't afford to live elsewhere on her meager salary.

"Thank you for walking with me," she said. "I do appreciate it."

He smiled a little. "It was my pleasure, Miss Dillon."

"Please, call me Biddy."

"Biddy." He said it so softly, as if her very common and ordinary name were special. "A fine goodnight to you. I hope someday you find your garden home."

"And I hope you find your land."

He stood on the walk while she climbed the steps to the front door. Lights burned inside, she not being the only one whose job kept her away until late hours. At the door, she turned back. He was there yet.

She offered a small wave. He answered with a nod. He didn't leave until she was fully inside. It was an unlooked-for kindness that she greatly appreciated. She knew very little about Ian, but the more time she spent with him, the more desperately she wanted to make his better acquaintance.

The next night when she reached the O'Connors' turnoff, Ian was there again.

"You're back." Her surprise added a tone of accusation she hadn't intended.

He only nodded. "You're still walking home alone, and this is still a dangerous city."

His brother and sister had already turned down their street and were quickly disappearing from view. For reasons she couldn't entirely explain, she didn't, and hadn't ever, felt truly uneasy in Ian's company. A bit shy, perhaps, and she blushed more than she cared to. But all in all, he was a comforting and reassuring presence. For all that, though, she couldn't be selfish.

"You go to the factory hours before most everyone," she said. "You'll be up long before the sun. You ought to be sleeping."

"What I ought to be is moving. I'm fair certain my feet are frozen to this spot."

She hadn't considered the impact of waiting for her in the cold. "You're tired *and* chilled to the bone. I—"

"Biddy." The lamplight illuminated his wide, laughing grin and the twinkle it brought to his dark eyes. "I like to tease. 'Tis a family trait, in fact. You'd be safe to assume that's what I'm doing when I say ridiculous things."

Good heavens, that smile of his set her heart fluttering. "I will try to remember that."

"We've a bit of a walk, and we'd do well to get started." He motioned for her to begin their journey.

"This is very kind of you." She walked alongside him. "You hardly know me, after all."

"This seems as good a way as any to get to know you better."

"As good as any?" She shook her head at that bit of logic. "Losing sleep to make an unnecessary walk down frigid streets in the dark of night? You call that 'good'?"

"Aye. A favorite undertaking of mine, to be sure."

Laughter bubbled inside, something she rarely experienced. "This is more of your teasing, is it?"

"If I tell you that I enjoyed our walk last night and am thoroughly enjoying this one so far, will you believe me when I say that I'm here because I want to be, and that you needn't worry that you're putting me out?" His tone was still cheerful but more earnest now.

"I suppose I'm not accustomed to people seeking out my company." She tucked her scarf more closely about her neck. "I'll likely prove a very boring companion."

"My favorite kind," he declared.

For the first time in she didn't know how long, Biddy laughed out loud. "You really do tease, it seems."

He chuckled along with her. "Likely more than I should."

"I like it, especially after a difficult day."

He looked over at her as they walked on. "You've had a difficult time of it?"

"Mr. Hunt still despises me." She slid her hands into her pockets. "Your brother said it's the misery of thick whiskers making him grumpy."

"I'd wager 'tis the misery of being an insufferable brute combined with an utter lack of sense."

"A rather unfortunate combination." She appreciated his ability to lighten the mood without making light of her situation.

44

'Twas a difficult balance to strike. "I'll admit, I worry throughout every day that my machine will seize up again, and he'll blame me for it. If not for you the last time, he'd've fired me, I know it."

"How is your machine running?" His question rang with sincere concern.

"I don't think it's ever run so well. Smooth as anything."

"And that's not enough to stop your worrying?"

She tried to ease the tension from her shoulders, but neither stretching them nor rolling them helped in the least. "I don't know enough about the machines to foresee problems. What if something goes wrong?"

"One gear had a worn tooth, but I replaced it. A bit of grease made a difference as well. I'll make whatever repairs are needed when I check it each morning."

"You check all the machines so often?" How could he possibly? There were hundreds and hundreds.

"Only the ones I'm concerned about."

Her heart thudded. "There's reason to worry about mine?"

"Mr. Hunt's willingness to use it as a weapon against you makes it a concern." The look he gave her, one of compassion and fondness, sent warmth swimming over her. Ian O'Connor possessed an unmistakable goodness.

"Thank you." The two words emerged nearly breathless. Her confusion and surprise wouldn't allow for anything else.

"'Tis my very real pleasure, Biddy." They'd reached the boarding house. "You rest and try not to worry over Mr. Hunt. I'll have your machine running well in the morning."

He was as good as his word. Every morning her machine whirred without a hint of trouble, and every night, he met her at the corner and saw her safely home.

They talked as they made their way down the dark, quiet streets, passing beneath the flickering gas lamps and over the cobblestones. She learned more about his life before America, more about his hopes for his new life here. He even managed to get her to speak a little of her own experiences, something she seldom did. Ian showed himself to have a fine sense of humor and a knack for making her laugh, but he also knew when to be more solemn, when to speak comfortingly instead of jokingly.

She liked him more with every walk they took. In fact, she found herself more than merely *liking* him. She didn't know what came next or what she was meant to do with these new feelings.

Her mother was no longer there to advise her. Though she'd forged something of a friendship with the other women in the boarding house, theirs wasn't a close association. She spent so much of her energy during the day trying to prove her worth as a worker that she'd not made any connections with her fellow boarders.

She was embarking on a new and unfamiliar path, and she hadn't the first idea what to do or where it led. She felt certain of only one thing: she deeply hoped Ian O'Connor would always be at the corner. *Their* corner.

Chapter Six

Ma smiled at Ian from the other side of the washbasin after dinner. "'Tis a fine thing having you help me these past evenings, but, my dear boy, you truly ought to be sleeping."

Though he was utterly exhausted, the thought of not walking Biddy home each night landed like lead on his heart. He couldn't like the idea of her being alone after dark in this too-often dangerous city. But it was more than that. From their earliest interactions, he'd suspected she was exactly the sort of woman he could fall madly and unchangingly in love with. He couldn't bear the thought of not seeing her every day.

"I worry for you," Ma went on. "You're running yourself to exhaustion keeping late nights when you have early mornings." She stopped in the midst of wiping a bowl clean and held his gaze firmly. "You cannot do this forever."

"Neither can I allow her to be in danger."

Ma watched him a touch too closely for comfort. She had a

knack for sorting out secrets, and he didn't mean to give this one away entirely. She'd likely sorted most of the mystery already.

"Would you leave Ciara to make that dark walk all on her own?" he asked.

"No, but Ciara is not a chance-met stranger." Ma ever had been in possession of a sharp mind. "So you must not consider Biddy a mere acquaintance."

He wasn't fooled by the way she pretended to once again be very interested in the plate she was scrubbing. Ma was rooting about for information.

"I am a chivalrous sort of fellow," he answered. "I can't resist a call for protection."

"Did she ask you to do this, then?" Ma handed him the plate to dry.

"She didn't." He wiped at it. "In fact, she gave many the same arguments, telling me that I was a fool to not be sleeping and looking after my own interests rather than hers."

"But you kept at it?"

He set the plate on its shelf, then crossed to Ma's side. "I was raised to be a good man, and a good man looks after the people he cares for, no matter the cost to himself." He kissed Ma's cheek. "Now wish me luck. I'm off to slay some New York dragons."

He'd not reached the door before she called earnestly after him. "Is she worthy of you, Ian?"

The question in his mind had long been the opposite. How could he, a man with little education, a dim future, a job that barely kept a roof over their heads, hardly a cent to his name, and no great gift for expressing himself, possibly be worthy of a woman he firmly suspected was closer to an actual angel than any other person he knew?

The question didn't answer itself by the time he stepped out onto the walk in front of their tenement building. The night was cold, the wind brutal. November was marching along, announcing louder with each day that winter followed swift on its heels, and that it promised to be punishing and harsh.

Of late, the elements mirrored the very feel of the city. The recent election had fallen in favor of Mr. Lincoln, an outcome hailed by the states in the north but met with great displeasure by those in the south. How, they argued, could they consider themselves a part of a country led by a man who so wholly represented a view of this nation that stood at odds with their own? And yet, the northern states countered, how could they have countenanced the election of a candidate who stood for a view of the country that they, themselves, found reprehensible? The divide only seemed to be growing.

Da had spoken of the political atmosphere as they'd walked to the factory. He'd taken an interest in the affairs of their new country from the beginning. Da's determination to know all he could of America had told Ian early on that the family would not be returning home. Da was finding his place in America, so they'd all do well to follow suit.

Yet that morning on their walk to work, it had been Patrick who'd spoken the most strongly about the state of the nation. He fell firmly in the camp of the northern states, speaking with great passion about the issues pulling the country apart. He, who generally laughed and joked about all manner of things, had been utterly solemn. 'Twas a change in his brother Ian had yet to make sense of.

When he stopped at the corner where he always met Biddy, he tried to push thoughts of upheaval and worry from his mind, but couldn't entirely manage it. Something heavy hung on the horizon; he could sense it.

A few more deep breaths, a few more pointed rejections of his dismal thoughts, and he had himself a bit more under control. He'd not mar his precious time in Biddy's company with melancholy thoughts.

Distant voices told him the factory workers were on their way home. Only Tavish, Ciara, and Biddy came this far. Ian leaned a shoulder against the gas streetlamp and waited.

His conversation with Biddy the night before had been almost entirely about his family. Tonight, he meant to ask her about hers. She seldom spoke of her family, though she'd once indicated that she was on her own. Had her parents passed on, or simply moved on? And how long had she been alone? His heart ached at the thought of her being lonely. He couldn't imagine what he would do without his family nearby.

Not far in the distance, Ciara and Tavish passed beneath a lamp. Ian looked behind them for signs of Biddy. He didn't see her. They wouldn't have abandoned her. Perhaps she was simply walking slowly? He'd been at the corner long enough that he couldn't have missed her if she'd been ahead of them.

"Where's Biddy?" he asked his siblings as they approached.

His sister looked up at him, her face pale and her eyes wide. Ian's heart dropped at the sight.

"Ciara?" he pressed.

"There was an accident," she whispered.

Icy dread dripped through him at those four words. "What—what happened?" He could hardly get the question out whole.

"She was reaching into—she had to. Mr. Hunt—he's been terrible. She had to do what she was told or—"

Ian turned to Tavish, hoping for an explanation that made sense. "What happened?"

"Machine tore her arm up," he said. "'Twasn't more than an hour ago. Seeing as she's too injured to work, she was fired. I saw her on her way out. It looked bad, Ian. Terrible bad."

Ian could hardly catch his breath. Biddy was hurt—badly, from the sound of it. She might've been in any state at all. He needed to find her. "She'd've gone to the boarding house, wouldn't she?"

Ciara and Tavish both nodded.

Ian ran. He ran as fast as his legs would carry him, his mind swimming with hundreds of terrible possibilities. What if the injury was even worse than Tavish had guessed? What if she was in agony? Or dying? What if she'd not had the strength to reach the boarding house? Would he even be able to find her?

He choked on his own thick breath as he turned onto her street. He didn't know which room was hers or where to find her, but he'd demand answers until he did. He had to see her. Had to help her.

The front door of the boarding house stood wide open. A tall, unkempt woman stepped out and tossed a carpet bag onto the dirt path leading to the road before disappearing inside once more.

In the next instant, Ian spotted Biddy sitting on a front step facing the street, leaning against the rickety bannister. She didn't seem to notice him or the woman or the bag.

He rushed to her, dropping to his knees on the ground in front of her, reassuring himself that she was there and alive. She sat hunched over, almost entirely hidden in shadow. The dim light from the streetlamp and what little spilled out of the boarding house only just illuminated her face. She was white as milk. Her eyes had taken on a glassy expression, as if not quite seeing the world around her.

"Biddy?" he said gently. "Talk to me, Biddy."

"I've lost my position," she whispered.

"I know, love."

"Mrs. Garrety won't allow me to stay without a job." She spoke weakly. 'Twas more than emotional exhaustion at having had a difficult day. Everything about her, from her pallor to her posture, spoke of quickly draining strength.

Tavish had said 'twas Biddy's arm that'd been injured, though Ian couldn't see well enough to know the extent.

"May I see your arm?" he asked.

She didn't answer, didn't meet his eye.

"Please, Biddy. I want to help."

She sat up straight enough to reveal her right arm, wrapped thickly in what looked like strips of cloth. Someone had offered some degree of help.

Ian couldn't see it well at all. He touched her arm as carefully as he could. She made the tiniest gasp of pain.

"I am sorry, dear." He didn't want to hurt her, but he

needed some idea of the state of her injury. He raised her arm ever so little, just enough for the dim light spilling through the boarding house windows to illuminate it.

Blood. Merciful heavens. The bandages were covered in bright red blood. Her dress was stained as well. *Saints above.* She watched him, concern etched into the lines of her face. He wouldn't add to her worries by showing his own. He squared his shoulders and kept his calm.

"Are you strong enough to walk?" he asked.

"Where would I go?" Her eyes, still faded with weakness, took on a desperate light. "Where would I go?"

"You're coming home with me. I'll not leave you here at the mercy of these vultures."

She didn't react in any way. The pain must have been overwhelming. He set himself on her uninjured left side, then slid his arm around her waist and helped her to her feet. She was weak, and, he ventured, growing quickly more so. To his utter relief, she didn't lean overly heavily on him. She had the strength to stand.

They moved slowly. The carpetbag Mrs. Garrety had tossed onto the front walk was there still. "This is yours?" he asked.

She nodded. Ian took the bag in his free hand, and they continued on.

"Do you know which part of the machine injured you?"

She took a shaky breath. "I don't know. Something sharp . . ." Her voice trailed off, though whether with misery at the memory or the pain, he couldn't say.

He hoped her injuries were only cuts, and that her arm

hadn't been crushed. 'Twas a necessarily slow journey back to the family flat. Biddy remained upright, but quiet. By the time they reached the tenement building the O'Connors' called home, Biddy's steps were dragging and her posture had slumped further. Thank the heavens the family lived on the ground floor.

When they arrived, Ma was waiting at the door. She didn't look the least surprised. Ciara and Tavish must have told her when they arrived home. "Set her on Ciara's bed," Ma said. "I've needle and thread waiting."

He dropped Biddy's bag inside the door, then lifted her fully into his arms, carrying her across the room. Ciara's bed was the only one outside Da and Ma's bedroom. The brothers all slept in the same room she did, but on the floor behind hanging quilts, Ian and Patrick in their corner and Tavish in another.

"Ciara told you what happened?" Ian asked.

"She mostly cried," Ma said. "Tavish explained what he knew." She lowered her voice. "How bad is her arm?"

"I've not seen the wound, but the dressing is fully soaked."

He laid Biddy down. She'd not spoken much in the last few minutes, though she'd held herself as strongly as ever. He eyed her worsening pallor with growing concern.

"What do you need me to do?" he asked Ma without taking his eyes off Biddy.

"I need you to give the lass a kiss or a sweet word or whatever you've established is appropriate between the two of you. Then I need you to go to bed."

"Ma—"

His protest was cut off immediately. "It won't do for you to lose your position as well. Come morning, she'll need your strength, and we'll need your wages to help bring her back to health. Both of those things require that you rest tonight."

"I don't want to be a burden," Biddy's whisper broke with emotion. "I am so sorry."

"Hush, sweetie." Ma spoke with maternal kindness. "You're no burden, I swear it. If Ian hadn't brought you back, I'd've gone to fetch you myself."

"I'm sorry," she whispered again.

Ma turned to Ian. "Set her thoughts at ease so she can rest. I'll be back in a moment to inspect the state of things."

Alone with Biddy—or as alone as one could be in cramped and crowded quarters—Ian knelt beside the low, rickety bed. He took her good hand in his, searching for the right words.

She, however, spoke first. "Your Ma is right, Ian. You need to sleep."

"As do you, Biddy."

Her next breath shook a little. "I don't know that I can. I hurt so much. And I'm being such a burden."

"I'll strike a deal with you, then." He held her worryingly vague gaze. "I will go lie down on m'bed and do my utmost to sleep, if you will promise to do the same."

She managed the smallest whisper of a smile. He raised her hand to his lips and kissed it.

"Ma will look after you. We all will." He stood. "Now, rest and heal. I'll see you tomorrow."

"Ian," she said when he'd taken but a single step away.

"Yes, Biddy?"

"Thank you."

He nodded and managed an expression of pleasure, though his heart had dropped a bit. He was grateful for her thank you, he truly was. But only after those two words had dropped from her lips had he realized that they were not the words he most wanted to hear.

Chapter Seven

Biddy had few clear memories of the previous night. The only detail she could recall with any clarity was Ian walking beside her, keeping her warm and upright. In the time since she'd awoken at the O'Connors' home, she'd slowly begun piecing the rest together.

Mrs. O'Connor had tended to her, and she was the one Biddy suspected had sewn her arm back together. The rest of the large family managed to go about their necessary routine despite Biddy's having disrupted it. She'd had food to eat, a bit of some kind of concoction for her pain, and a place to rest and sleep. What she hadn't had was even a moment of Ian's company.

He is at the factory, she reminded herself. He left so early that there would not have been an opportunity to see him. She ought not to selfishly hope for more of his time when he'd already sacrificed so many hours of sleep to walk her home these past weeks.

Biddy sat on the bed, blankets tucked around her,

enveloped in the relative quiet of the almost-empty O'Connor flat as the afternoon waned. It wasn't an idle quiet, but a peaceful one. The bed she occupied sat pushed up against a wall, not far from a window. The youngest of the O'Connor children, a little boy of not more than five or six, lay on the floor on his belly, playing with a roughly carved wooden animal—a horse or dog. Mrs. O'Connor sat nearby, working on a pile of mending. A pot of soup hung over glowing embers in the fireplace, awaiting the family's return.

The O'Connors were a family devoted to one another; she'd seen that truth when she'd called on the family weeks earlier. She'd envied them then. A part of her still did. These O'Connors, she'd wager, would move heaven and earth for one another.

So unlike her own family. She didn't know all the details of her parents' story, but only one of two tales could be true: either her mother had abandoned her father at the height of their suffering, or her father had sent them far away, only to turn his back and forget them. No matter the truth of it, one of them had deserted the other. There had been no abiding connection, no loyalty.

Mrs. O'Connor broke the silence between them, offering Biddy a welcome excuse to leave behind her heavy thoughts. "You seem to be feeling better this afternoon."

"I am, and I have you and your family to thank for that."

"Now don't you start apologizing again because you think you're a burden." Mrs. O'Connor spoke with amusement, not with anger or frustration. "That was near about the only thing you said last night, over and over again, how sorry you were."

"Did I at least thank you?"

"Aye."

That one word brought up a question that had lingered in Biddy's mind as she'd come to know Ian a little better. "I've always understood *aye* to be a rather Scottish word, but I've heard both you and Ian use it."

Mrs. O'Connor grinned broadly. "You've stumbled upon a secret of mine, Biddy. I am not Irish."

That couldn't possibly be true. Her manner of speaking, other than that one rogue word, was indistinguishable from the many, many Irishmen all around them.

"I can see I've surprised you." Mrs. O'Connor picked out a seam in a dress as she spoke. "I was born in the Highlands, where my family had lived since time began. But the man who owned the land we called home decided he'd do better to use it for grazing his sheep."

"A clearance." Biddy had heard tale of such things amongst her Irish neighbors.

"A rather plain word for such a brutal thing, is it not?" Her expression held a heavy note of sadness. "But, yes, it was a clearance. Some of those tossed aside remained nearby, seeking out what living they could find. Some moved south to bigger cities in search of work. Some, I imagine, set their sights on America and all the good fortune this place promised."

This was supposed to have been a land of opportunity, but it hadn't lived up to the reputation in many ways.

"My family," Mrs. O'Connor continued, "sailed to Ireland and settled in County Antrim. I was not much older than

Finbarr, here. I quickly adapted to the Irish way of being and speaking, just as Finbarr has taken on an American manner of speaking, simply from hearing it when we're about the city or when he goes with me to do my cleaning work.

"Though she is not truly my motherland, Ireland will always be my home. Few things cling to me from my earliest days in Scotland, but using *aye* is one of them. And it's not so foreign to Irishmen in general that they've shown themselves uncomfortable with it. Some even say it themselves, you know. Especially those from Ulster."

"I hail from County Mayo," Biddy said.

Mrs. O'Connor smiled broadly. "A Connacht lass, are you?"

"I don't remember much of Ireland. I was forced to leave at about Finbarr's age."

Mrs. O'Connor sighed. "But it's still in your heart, isn't it?"

"Always."

"Always," Mrs. O'Connor agreed.

A quick knock sounded from the door.

"Who do you suppose that could be?" Mrs. O'Connor wondered aloud.

"It could be robbers," little Finbarr announced from his position on the floor.

Mrs. O'Connor nodded solemnly as she stood. "I will be certain to check first."

"Good." Finbarr returned, apparently unconcerned, to his play.

Mrs. O'Connor inched the door open, peeked outside, then turned back to face her little boy. "Why, it's not robbers at all,

Finbarr. It's Maura." She opened the door fully, revealing a young woman with a baby on her hip.

Biddy felt certain this new arrival had been among the family on that Sunday evening. Either a daughter or daughter-in-law, she'd wager.

"What brings you 'round, Maura?" Mrs. O'Connor motioned her inside.

"I'm needing to run down to the market, and I know you're not cleaning anywhere today. I'd hoped you might watch Aidan for me."

"Of course." Mrs. O'Connor lifted the baby into her arms. "This wee bundle is welcome any time."

Maura's gaze fell on Biddy. "You've a visitor, it seems."

"You remember Ian's friend, the one he showed his bare chest to before running from the room like a frightened rabbit?"

"Remember? How could I forget?" Maura's dark eyes danced with laughter. "I've never seen the poor man as red as he was in that moment. I'd've felt badly for him if it hadn't been so terribly funny." She crossed to the bed. "Your name's Biddy, if I remember correctly."

"Yes. Biddy Dillon."

"She's had an accident at the factory," Mrs. O'Connor said, bouncing the baby in her arms.

"I am sorry to hear that." Maura sat on the edge of the bed. "Those factories are dangerous. I was so relieved when my Grady found work elsewhere. I worried for him so fiercely each day."

Unbidden came the memory of Ian reaching down into the spinning machine, the very one that had torn her arm to bits.

He worked with all the machines, great lurking beasts capable of crushing all of him. Biddy tried to push back the thought, but it refused to be entirely dismissed.

"Might I fetch you something from the market?" Maura asked Biddy. "Anything you're in need of?"

Biddy could have used any number of things, but she had no means of paying for so much as an apple. "No, I thank you."

Maura turned enough to face her mother-in-law once more. "Anything you're needing?"

"Only some time with this wee grandbaby of mine." Mrs. O'Connor cooed at the little one.

"Then you'll have it." Maura crossed back toward the door. She kissed her son. "Thank you again," she said to Mrs. O'Connor. "And, Biddy, I hope you're feeling better soon." She waved to the room, wished Finbarr a fond farewell, and slipped out again.

Though that brief encounter was the entirety of Biddy's interaction with Maura, she found that she liked the woman. Indeed, she liked all of the O'Connors.

The littlest of the bunch was even then climbing up onto the bed beside her.

"Mind her arm, Finbarr," Mrs. O'Connor instructed. "She's hurt it, you'll remember."

The lad moved with utmost care, his face pulled in a look of deep concentration. Bless him, he was being as mindful as he knew how. She sat in bed with her injured arm on the side next to the wall, which offered it some protection from accidental bumps. Still, she kept her arm tucked protectively next to her.

He crawled to the head of the bed and sat directly beside her on her uninjured side.

"A good day to you, Finbarr," Biddy said.

"I have a horse." He held up his toy.

"Does your horse have a name?"

"No." Finbarr shook his head. "But Tavish says he must have a name to be a proper horse."

"Perhaps you should name the horse 'Tavish.'"

The lad giggled long and loud. Mrs. O'Connor's laughter joined in from across the room. Finbarr crawled all over the foot of the bed, making his horse gallop on the quilt. He looked back at her regularly, flashing a grin every time. Biddy cradled her arm against herself to keep it from being jostled. Though the lad's play was adding to her discomfort and even causing the occasional jolt of pain, she didn't want him to leave. Mrs. O'Connor cooed to her little grandson, moving now and then to the window and looking out, no doubt anticipating the return of her family, though the earliest arrivals would not leave the factory for at least an hour more.

This was a loving family and a joyful one, precisely the kind Biddy had always longed to have. For these brief moments, she was part of their lives, and it did her heart a world of good. She forced herself not to think of how much lonelier she would be when she was healed and on her own again. There would be time enough for worrying about that.

"You've grown pale," Mrs. O'Connor said. "Is your arm paining you again?"

It was, in fact, and she admitted as much.

"I'll give you a bit more of the powders, though they'll make you sleepy."

"Sleep will do me good."

Mrs. O'Connor gave her a look of kindness, and concern, and tenderness, which put her instantly in mind of her own mother in times of illness and worry. Biddy missed her mother terribly.

"I'll just place this sweet bundle beside you." Mrs. O'Connor set the sleeping baby beside Biddy, snuggled up against her left side, next to the arm that wasn't paining her. "Give me a moment."

Finbarr crawled toward her again and sat beside the baby. He watched him sleep, seemingly fascinated. "Babies are very little," he said.

"Yes, they are." Biddy said. "You were once this small, Finbarr. Can you believe it?"

He shook his head, eyes wide with amazement. "How do you know that?"

"I am very clever."

He tipped his head to one side and smiled bashfully. "I like you, Biddy." With those four words, the tiny boy won her heart. "Can you stay with us?"

"For a time, sweet Finbarr. For a time." How she wished she could promise more, for her sake even more than his.

Mrs. O'Connor gave her the powders, then took up the baby once more. "Come along, you imp," she said to Finbarr. "Let Biddy sleep."

"I won't keep her awake," he said. "I'll be quiet and still."

He received a look of deepest doubt from his mother. "You'll wiggle about and keep her from resting."

"I won't, Ma. Please?" How could anyone resist that dear little face?

"He could stay a bit," Biddy said. "Just a few minutes more."

"You'll hold very still?" Mrs. O'Connor asked.

Finbarr nodded.

"And you'll not talk her ear off?"

He nodded once more.

"Very well." She surrendered with a sigh. "Only a little while, mind you."

Biddy lowered herself to lay flat once more. Finbarr curled up next to her, atop the blankets. The briefest of moments passed before he spoke.

"Are you asleep yet?"

She smiled to herself. "Not yet, lad."

"I could sing you a song. Ma sings to me when I can't sleep."

"You'd sing to me?"

"I would play my whistle too, but Ma says it sounds like a bird wishing for death."

Biddy bit back a laugh, sensing that he wouldn't understand why the remark was funny, but might, instead, be hurt by such a response. "Singing sounds like the perfect thing to help me sleep."

"You have to close your eyes, though."

She did as she was bidden.

Soft as a whisper of a breeze, he began to sing a song she knew all too well. A heartbreaking and lonesome air she'd heard time and again.

Smiling, beguiling, cheering, endearing,
Together how oft o'er the mountains we strayed,
By each other delighted and fondly united,
I have listened all day to my dear Irish Boy.

He sang the chorus again and again, his voice growing slower and quieter with each repetition. He was lulling himself to sleep, the dear thing.

Biddy set her good arm around him and tucked him up close. Her gaze fell on Mrs. O'Connor watching from the rocker across the room.

"Thank you for being kind to Finbarr," she said. "He often feels overlooked, being so much younger than the others."

"'Tis my pleasure. And thank you for letting me be part of a family again, even if only for a little while. I haven't had that in ever so long."

Mrs. O'Connor nodded. "Now close your eyes as the boy instructed. Rest your weary soul."

Her soul was indeed weary, but she'd found in this small, humble home, a balm for the aching deep inside her heart.

Chapter Eight

When Ian left for work that morning, Biddy had still been sleeping. Leaving her, not knowing if her health was yet in danger or if she was truly on the mend, not having the chance to say so much as a word to her, had been torturous. He'd spent the entire day thinking of her and worrying about her.

He could not entirely clear his mind of the sight of the blood-soaked bandages. Ma hadn't allowed him the slightest glimpse of her arm beneath that horrifying mass of red cloth. He'd spent every waking moment since then imagining the worst.

What if she'd bled too much to regain her strength? What if she'd forever lost the use of her arm? What if her wounds turned putrid?

The sooner he found out if she was well, the sooner he'd be able to breathe again.

After their shift ended, Patrick must've sensed his anxiety, because they'd not taken more than a few steps beyond the factory gates when the blasted lad started laughing. "Off with you, Ian, before you have a stroke. Go see to your sweet lass."

"She's not *my* sweet lass."

His brother only laughed harder. "Run home. It'll do you far more good than jumping clear out of your skin with worry."

"Won't you miss me terribly if I abandon you?"

Patrick shot him the driest of looks. "'Twill be a misery, to be sure. However, I'll be walking past the bakery. I believe I'll find solace there."

"Fond of bread, are you?"

"Incredibly fond . . ." Patrick grinned. "Of the baker's daughter."

"I thought you were in pursuit of the lass who sells flowers on the corner."

He shook his head. "We're only friends."

"You have a lot of friends."

"And a lot of brothers." He slapped a hand on Ian's shoulder. "But you're my favorite."

"Of course I am."

His brother shoved him in the direction of home. "Away with you. We've both a fair bit of wooing to do. Go."

Ian managed the journey faster than he'd ever thought possible. He all but flew up the front stairs. At the doorway to their flat, he stopped long enough to pull himself together.

He calmly opened the door. Ma sat in her rocking chair, mending. She didn't look worried or mournful.

"Biddy?" he asked, hoping he'd kept his panic tucked out of sight.

"She spent most of the day resting," Ma said. "She puts on a brave face, but there's pain in her eyes."

"She was awake, then?" That seemed a good sign. He stepped closer to Ciara's bed. Biddy slept soundly, though her features were not entirely devoid of pain. She was also not without company. A little boy, his ginger hair jutting out in all directions, lay curled up next to her. "What is Finbarr doing up here?"

Ma smiled. "Sweet boy has stars in his eyes for the lass. He sang her a song so she could sleep."

"Did it work?"

"Yes, but *he* fell asleep first. He woke up last night while I was tending to the lass and never could fall back to sleep. The dear thing is exhausted. Both of them are, really."

They were both sleeping now, though. "Biddy didn't mind his attentions and intrusions?"

"Not in the least." Ma set her mending aside. She moved to the bed, gazing lovingly on her little boy. "I've wanted to move him to his trundle, give them both a better chance of resting deeply. But I feared I'd only wake her in the trying."

"I'll move him."

He bent over the bed, careful not to jostle it at all. Biddy's good arm was wrapped around little Finbarr. Ian gently slipped his hand beneath hers, ignoring the tug on his heart, and lifted her hand and arm. He set it carefully on the bed, but kept their fingers entwined for a drawn-out moment.

"You can just set him on the trundle," Ma repeated.

"Aye." He knew the unnecessary repetition for what it was: a light scold for being distracted from his task.

Ian lifted Finbarr from the bed and into his arms. The boy awoke enough to reach back toward the bed.

"You've your own bed, lad," Ian reminded him. "Biddy has claim on this one."

"I left Tavish," Finbarr said groggily.

"He means his little horse." Ma pointed to the wooden toy.

Ian shifted Finbarr to one arm and retrieved the horse with his free hand. "Weeks of refusing to choose a name for the ugly thing, and he picked 'Tavish'?"

Ma returned to her rocker. "He told Biddy that Tavish had been taunting him for not having named his horse, so she suggested that 'Tavish' would be a good choice."

Ian bit back the laugh that immediately rose to the surface, not wanting to wake either of the poor, exhausted souls. Finbarr, gripping his horse, had grown heavy against his shoulder again. Biddy hadn't moved even the tiniest bit.

"She has a fine sense of humor." Ian couldn't seem to take his eyes off her.

"I know. We had a great deal of time today for talking."

"Then she's doing well? Her arm's healing?"

Ma nodded. "Quite well. A terrible number of cuts on that arm of hers, and they'll ache her for a good while. But she'll be in fine fettle given some time."

Ian carried Finbarr to Ma and Da's small bedroom off the main living space, where Finbarr's tiny trundle awaited him. He set the boy down and tucked a blanket about his shoulders.

Finbarr's eyes fluttered open. He smiled up at Ian. "Biddy named my horse."

"I heard."

The little lad sighed and closed his eyes again. "I love her. We should keep her forever and ever."

"I don't know that she'd stay," Ian whispered.

Finbarr was asleep again. *Dear boy.* He'd been a light in all their lives these past five years. They'd left Ireland with such heavy and aching hearts, hope having all but died in the Famine, and America having proven incapable of resurrecting it. But this lad, this joyful, kind, loving little boy, had brought that hope back to the family. Somehow they had to find a way to give him a better future than daily walks to and from a factory, with endless hours inside its dark and dangerous walls.

From the room beyond came the sound of the front door opening and Patrick's jovial voice asking if Ian had rushed inside and swept "the girl" off her feet.

Ian stepped into sight at once and folded his arms across his chest. "I thought you were wooing the baker's daughter."

Patrick sighed dramatically. "Alas, she wasn't available, and neither was my flower lass or any of my other friends." He hung his coat on its usual nail. "Seems I'm the only one done with work this early in the day who isn't old like you."

"This 'old person' has vigor enough to belt you in the gob, brother."

A quiet voice very near Ian spoke. "That seems unnecessarily violent."

Biddy. He turned toward the bed. Heavens, she was still so pale. She needed to rest. "Did Patrick wake you?"

"Please say no," Patrick requested, laughter heavy in his tone. "He'll kick m' teeth out otherwise."

"He didn't wake me. My arm did."

Ian sat on the edge of the bed, eying the thick layers of linen wrapped protectively around her right arm. He didn't see any blood seeping through. Ma had clearly taken pains to keep the bandaging fresh and clean. "Is it paining you?"

"Something awful."

Ian looked over his shoulder at Ma. "Have we any powders?"

"She'll not be wanting them until after she's eaten. Elsewise, they'll not stay where they're meant to."

That was sensible. "I'll fetch her some supper."

Patrick spoke almost before Ian had finished his declaration. "I'll fetch her food. After all, I owe the lass a kindness for not getting me belted."

Biddy smiled a little, but 'twas a shaky, difficult movement, as if the effort only added to her misery.

"What can I do for you, Biddy? I hate seeing you so pained."

She took a slow breath. Her posture and belabored movements spoke of bone-deep weariness.

"You've done so much for me already, Ian. I don't know what would've become of me last night if not for you."

Though he wasn't usually so bold, he took her hand in his. "Have you no one you might've turned to?"

"Not a soul."

In that moment, his heart broke for her. Even in his loneliest times, through his most difficult challenges in life, Ian had never truly been alone. He had his family. Biddy, it seemed, had no one.

"Although . . ." Her tone lightened unexpectedly. Her

expression grew the tiniest bit less burdened. "Finbarr did say that he likes me, so I suppose I do have one ally in this world."

"Actually . . . " Ian bent closer. "Finbarr said he *loves* you, which I'd say makes him more than a mere ally. He's your champion now. He'll not ever allow you to be alone." Fearing he'd allowed too much of his own wishes to enter that declaration, Ian retreated once more into friendly, teasing conversation. "That means, of course, you'll likely not have another moment's peace in all the time you're here, and you'll be forced to find names for every disfigured wood carving the lad can lay claim to."

Biddy turned a little on her side, looking more directly at him. "Will Tavish be terribly upset that we named the horse after him?"

"Aye." Ian chuckled. "And he'll make a grand show of being offended before making a joke of the whole thing." Tavish was an agreeable fellow, nearly as happy as little Finbarr.

She sighed—and it was a sound of contentment, not suffering. "I like your family, Ian O'Connor. Yours is precisely the kind I've always wished for—loving and loyal, and not the sort to abandon a person."

Abandon? A world of hurt lay in that one word.

"Quit jawing the colleen's ear off, Ian," Patrick called from across the room. "Let the poor lass eat, will you?"

"Is food your key to success with your horde of friends?" Ian tossed back.

"Obviously."

Ma came up behind Ian and spoke to Biddy from over his

shoulder. "Are you feeling strong enough to sit at the table? With only one arm, you'd struggle to feed yourself in bed."

"I may need a steadying arm," Biddy answered.

Ma gave Ian a nudge. "I believe our Ian'd be willing to provide that."

The short walk to the table put Ian's mind more at ease regarding her well-being. Though she did need a moment's help upon first standing, she moved entirely on her own strength the rest of the way. She was pained and weary, but she possessed a strong will.

"Go on ahead and eat," Ma told her.

Biddy thanked Ma for the meal, Patrick for fetching it for her, and Ian for helping her to the table. She asked about Finbarr and Da, Tavish and Ciara. Patrick took her interest as an opportunity to regale her with a number of increasingly ridiculous family stories. Though Biddy didn't laugh uproariously as some might have, she did seem to genuinely enjoy the entertainment.

Ian crossed to the pot hanging over the fire and ladled a bowl of soup for himself. Ma joined him at the fireplace.

"I like her, Ian," she said in a low voice. "Such a dear, sweet girl. I cannot countenance how terribly that overseer treated her. How could anyone be so unkind to such a tenderhearted lass?"

He bit back a few choice words he'd fashioned for Mr. Hunt. He was a brute, ever on the hunt for a new target. That he'd unleashed his venom on Biddy made him the worst sort of man.

Ian had investigated the matter that had led to Biddy's injury. The machine had been in full working order. Hunt's insistence that she reach into the machine in search of bits of

74

cotton, despite no indication that anything was lodged in the gears, hadn't come about for any reason other than cruelty.

Da, who met often enough with the factory owner to be known by name, had stayed behind to tell Mr. Grandford of the overseer's behavior. Nothing might come of it, but Ian wouldn't allow her suffering to go unacknowledged.

Yet he chose to focus on her recovery rather than let his thoughts linger on the cause of it. He'd be ill advised to let himself stew over it, lest he march back to the factory and let Mr. Hunt know just what he thought of the man. He'd lose his job, perhaps bring vengeance down on his siblings' heads as well, and then where would they all be?

"Biddy seems to be recovering." He made the observation as much as a reassurance to himself as an inquiry.

"Aye. She doesn't seem one to buckle under the weight of life, though clearly she's endured her share of difficulties." Ma glanced back at Biddy, who ate her soup as she listened to Patrick's continued stories. "She told me she's not had family in a long time and was ever so grateful to be included in this one, even for a short while. She must be terribly lonely."

Knowing now that she didn't have family of her own, he couldn't begrudge her that longing. But was the chance to be something of a daughter and sister to someone, even for a short while, the greatest pull she felt in this house?

Heavens, he hoped not.

Chapter Nine

Sunday arrived and Biddy was still at the O'Connors' home recovering. She'd slept so late that morning, the family was gone at mass when she'd awoken. Mrs. O'Connor had insisted that sleeping was an important part of her recovery, but to Biddy, it felt far too close to laziness.

Not wishing to be a burden, especially without having given the O'Connors anything in return, she attempted to do a bit of straightening, but she couldn't manage much with only one hand. And the brief effort rendered her bad arm even more tender than before.

She resigned herself to sitting in the rocking chair and waiting for the family's return, having yet to repay their kindness in any way. In time, she would be stronger. She'd help Mrs. O'Connor. Once she was healed enough, she would find work again so they needn't support her. She'd find a place of her own. Entirely on her own. Again.

Footsteps sounded on the landing outside the door. The

family was returning home. How she hoped they didn't resent her continued presence there.

The door opened. *Ian.* The sight of him brought an instant flood of relief, a sense of calm in her storm of uncertainty. Their eyes met, and he smiled. Saints, she'd come to love that tender smile.

He had not returned alone. Little Finbarr rushed across the room, directly to her. "Biddy! Biddy!" He leaned his elbows on her lap and looked up into her face. "We walked home so fast. And we played a game."

"What game did you play?" She adored conversations with this tiny ray of sunshine.

"Ian asked me silly questions, and I gave him silly answers."

Biddy rested her head in her upturned hand. "What questions did he ask you?"

"Before you answer," Ian jumped in, "I need to ask Miss Biddy how her arm feels." He snatched up a pile of clean fabric strips from the basket where Mrs. O'Connor kept them at the ready, then he pulled a chair up beside her.

"It's sore," she admitted. "More than it has been, but I did attempt to do more with it this morning than I have since being laid low. I'd imagine the soreness is the result of all that movement."

His look was one of deepest empathy. "Are you growing anxious to be up and about?"

"I am not accustomed to being so useless."

He carefully took hold of her injured arm, a ritual they'd come to know well. Every evening after returning from the factory, Ian undertook the task of replacing the bandaging. The conversations they'd previously enjoyed during their evening walks to her boarding house had resumed during this far less pleasant task. Yet despite the pain, she looked forward to those times each day.

As he unwrapped the strips of cloth, they tugged on her wounds. She sucked in a breath, trying to keep the pain hidden. The day before when she'd winced during his ministrations, Ian had looked so very guilty. She didn't wish for him to feel anything but appreciated for the kindnesses he showed her.

"Did I hurt you?" His brown eyes turned from his task to her face with a heartrending look of apology.

"'Tisn't too painful," she said.

One corner of his mouth twitched. "Have you taken to lying to me, Itty Biddy?"

He'd begun using the nickname these past few days. When she'd asked what it meant, he'd only shrugged. The name was an odd one, but something in the way he said it, the smile shining in his tone and his eyes, had made it a favorite of hers. He likely didn't mean for it to feel like *dear*, or *darlin*, or *sweetheart*, but it did. Heaven help her, it did.

"You'd best tell Miss Biddy all about our question game," Ian said to Finbarr. "She'll likely need the distraction."

"Because her arm hurts?"

"Her arm hurts terribly, lad."

Finbarr climbed onto Biddy's lap. She put her good arm around him and asked, "What questions did your brother ask you?"

"What is my favorite food with potatoes? Do I like my ginger hair?"

"Do you like your hair?"

Finbarr nodded enthusiastically. "We match."

"You and Ian, you mean?"

Finbarr nodded, then asked her, "Do you like my ginger hair?"

She lowered her voice as if sharing a great secret. "I like ginger hair very much." She glanced at Ian. He'd reddened a bit but otherwise didn't seem as though he'd overheard.

"Then Ian asked me what animal I'd want to be my friend." Finbarr pressed his hands over his mouth as he laughed. "I said a cow."

Biddy smiled despite the pain of Ian unwrapping her arm. She focused, instead, on Finbarr's joy-filled company.

"A cow would be a very fine friend, I'd wager," she said. "Do you have a name for your cow? If the horse got a name, the cow should as well."

Finbarr pressed his mouth together. His brow furrowed with deep concentration.

Ian's shoulders shook lightly with a silent laugh. "What's it to be, Finbarr? Shall we call it 'Colin the Cow' or 'Moo-reen'?"

Finbarr's eyes pulled wide. "We can call it Patrick!"

The brothers laughed, grinning at each other. They launched into an increasingly silly discussion on which animals each of their siblings should be named for, and where they'd keep their collection of oddly named pets. Ian's tenderness for the little boy was touching. She liked him all the more for it.

Biddy tucked the younger brother affectionately near while keeping her gaze on the elder.

He caught her staring at him and dropped his gaze immediately to her bandages again.

Finbarr leaned against her and sighed. "I am happy you are staying with us, but I am sad about your arm."

"Ian is taking very good care of my arm," she said. "And the two of you are making me very happy that I am here."

He didn't look up at her, but Biddy caught Ian's smile. How was it that bringing a bit of happiness to his face brought her such pleasure?

In the next moment, Ian pulled back the last of the bandages. The cold air stung as it assaulted the raw and broken skin.

"Does it appear putrid?" She couldn't bring herself to look.

"What it appears to be is sore. Perhaps a bit of time free of the tug of the bandages would help it heal faster."

His mother's careful stitches held the deepest of the cuts closed. None of them were discolored or oozing.

"I would enjoy not having it pulled on every time the bandaging is changed," she said.

"I didn't hurt you, did I?"

Heavens, but he sounded so guilty.

"A great lumbering machine hurt me, Ian O'Connor. You have been . . . wonderful."

"We should name a cat after you," Finbarr said. "It would be 'Itty Biddy Kitty.'"

Ian shot her a look of barely held back amusement. "That's an opportunity too good to miss, I'd say."

In the very next instant, the entire O'Connor clan, including those who no longer lived there, flooded inside, chatter and laughter filling the room. The family all inquired after her. Ciara teared up a bit at the sight of Biddy's sewn-together arm. Patrick, Grady, and Tavish spent the entirety of their first few minutes giving Ian a remarkably hard time, christening him "Doctor Ian." He took it in stride, doing a bit of jesting himself.

Mary, the oldest daughter, and Maura, their daughter-in-law, took up the task of preparing the family's meal while Mr. and Mrs. O'Connor cooed and cuddled their little grandbaby. The brothers and brother-in-law alternated between laughter and more solemn conversations. In the midst of it all, Finbarr remained cozily situated on her lap, and Ian sat in the chair directly beside her.

"Grady, love," Maura called over the jovial hum of voices. "Will you hang this pot over the fire for me?"

Grady hopped up without a moment's hesitation. "Anything at all for you, dear." He quickly kissed his wife before undertaking the task.

Such ready affection. Mr. and Mrs. O'Connor were similarly tender and devoted. Mary and Thomas exchanged little smiles and glances quite regularly as well. In all her days of wondering if people in love turned away from each other the way her parents had done, Biddy had never seen such sure proof of the opposite as she did amongst this family. The sight did her mind, heart, and soul a world of good.

"You seem to be pondering something pleasant," Ian said.

Warmth stole over her at the thought that he'd been watching her. "I was only thinking how very much your family loves each other. It is a fine sight to see. And a rare one."

"You're very fond of them." Something in the observation felt like a question.

"I am."

"I'd say they're rather fond of you as well." Why did he sound a bit unhappy about that? Surely he didn't wish for his family to dislike her.

"Begging your pardon, Biddy." Patrick had reached them; the room was not very large. "I'm here to steal away your company."

"You're taking Ian?" Almost of its own accord, her hand sought out his, needing the reassurance that he was still there.

Patrick shook his head firmly. "I'm not so brave as that, dearie. I've come for the wee little bean sprout."

Finbarr perked up. "Me?"

"Aye." Patrick ruffled the lad's hair. "Thomas wants you to fetch your whistle."

"We're to have music?" Finbarr asked as he climbed down from her lap.

"We are. And if you're a good lad, I'd wager the lot of us'll even dance with you."

"Grand!" Finbarr ran for the bedroom.

"He likes to dance, does he?" Biddy could easily picture the tiny ball of excitement spending his energy that way.

"Loves it," Patrick answered. "He'd've been absolutely blissful at the *céilís* back home. 'Tis a full shame we haven't room enough for a true Irish party here."

"What a joy it would be to have Irish food and music again. Stories. Dancing. Irish voices filling the air." The first tenement Biddy and her mother lived in upon arriving in America had been filled to overflowing with Irish. They'd managed a few *céilís* despite their limited space. "I've not enjoyed an Irish party in ages."

"O'Connors!" Patrick's voice rang out, grasping his family's attention. "Our Biddy, here, is in dire need of a *céilí*. 'Tis our duty as Irishmen to see to that she has one. What say all of you?"

The agreements were swift and enthusiastic. The room, which had already been busy, erupted in a flurry of activity.

Patrick turned back to face her. "We haven't the space to do justice to a true *céilí*, but I think you'll enjoy yourself all the same."

"'Our Biddy'?" She repeated his exact word choice, but with doubt clear in her tone.

"Oh, you're one of us, and no mistaking," he said. "We are all too fond of you to think otherwise."

She looked to Ian for confirmation.

He squeezed her fingers. "We are all excessively fond of you."

We. With that, some of the tug she'd felt in her heart loosened, replaced with an unexpected ache. She tried to hide her disappointment and confusion. Why should her spirits sag while having her hand held by a man she cared for as much as she did Ian?

"Begor, Ian," Patrick muttered. "You're such an idiot."

Finbarr reappeared clutching his penny whistle. "I found it."

"Good man," Patrick said. "Run it over to Thomas, then see if you can't steal that watch away from Tavish so he'll not be too distracted to sing with us."

Finbarr took up the task with eagerness. Patrick followed in his wake.

We are all fond of you. We. Ian's voice repeated in her head as the O'Connors began their music. *We.* That was the word sitting the most uncomfortably. Patrick had been speaking of the family's feelings for her. So, it seemed, had Ian.

He grinned as he sang along with the others, all but losing himself in the music. This was the lightest and happiest she'd seen him. Joy filled his expression even as a lump formed in her throat.

She'd wanted him to say "*I* am fond of you," rather than, "*We* are." But watching him, feeling the warmth of his hand holding hers, she knew even those exact words would have fallen short.

Mere *fondness* from Ian O'Connor would never be enough.

Chapter Ten

Biddy had put a wall between the two of them, and Ian was at a loss to know why. He'd thought he'd been making progress in proving his worth to her. She'd seemed pleased with his company, gifting him smiles and allowing him to hold her hand. How had things changed so quickly? And how could he possibly fix it, if he didn't know what had gone wrong?

Ian bent over a chair he was repairing, pretending not to overhear her conversation with Da, but in reality, listening intently for some hint as to what had happened to make her so distant.

"I remember very little of Ireland," she said. "Other than how green it was."

"As do we all. Anything else?"

Ian held his breath, not wanting to miss any glimpse of herself Biddy might offer.

"I remember my father's house."

Her *father's* and not her *family's*. Odd, that.

"His family must have been very wealthy. The house was the biggest I've ever seen. The walls were so high I couldn't see the tops. And the windows were high above even my mother's head. Row after row of windows."

"Imagine cleaning all that glass," Ma said, setting a bowl of colcannon before Da.

"I don't remember glass, only empty window wells. Not entirely empty, actually. They did have the bars that the panes of glass ought to have sat between." Biddy smiled a little, a sad, forlorn smile. "I'm likely remembering wrong. I was very young."

Ma patted her hand. "At least you remember something of those times with your father. That's a blessing."

Biddy's gaze dropped to her supper. She said nothing after that. Ma looked over at Ian, a question in her eyes.

He was at a loss. He'd long suspected that her family life had not been a happy one. However, he knew no details and therefore could offer no insights.

A stretch of silence pulled long between them. After a moment, Da spoke. "I was summoned to see Mr. Grandford today. He's heard of an opportunity and chose to tell me of it."

That was odd, indeed, and vague. Ian stepped away from the broken chair and moved closer to the table.

"He indicated a need for a large family," Da said. "A hardworking one, with some knowledge of working the land."

"Land?" Ma set down her spoon—her meal, it seemed, forgotten in a heartbeat.

Da nodded, the lines in his forehead creased with thought. "He hadn't any particulars yet, but I confess, hearing the words *opportunity, family,* and *land* all in the same conversation had me hoping for things I dare not set my heart on."

"Would this opportunity take us away from New York?" Patrick's dark brow creased too, though with worry.

"It would. Far from New York, in fact." Da pushed his bowl aside and folded his hands on the tabletop. "Mr. Grandford offered few details except to say that there is land for the getting."

Land of their own. Land far from the filthy air of the city. Far from the factory and its crushing, grinding machines. The family would no longer be cramped into a tiny tenement with little hope for more. Even if they couldn't manage a large house, they'd have the open space of the outdoors, with room to move and think and breathe.

"Land of our own, Thomas." Ma pressed her hand to her heart. "But do you think it a good offering?"

Da took an audible breath and turned, for the first time since sharing the news, toward his wife. "I think it might be."

Her smile quavered a bit. "We'd have room. And you'd have earth again, Thomas. You're never happier than when you have your own bit of earth."

He reached over and took Ma's hand in his. "That, my dear, is not entirely true. I care for a great many things more than dirt and sky and the wind against my face."

"Well, yes, you are very fond of colcannon."

Da laughed and returned to his meal.

The sound of a very badly played penny whistle emerged from the bedroom.

Some of Patrick's humor returned. "It seems Finbarr's awake."

"I'll fetch him." Biddy stood so quickly, and spoke so abruptly, that all eyes were suddenly on her. The conversation halted. She left the table hastily, moving with singular purpose to the bedroom door.

"Go after her," Ma said softly to Ian. "Speaking of her family brought her spirits low. I daresay she needs a bit of kindness about now."

He began his trek across the room before Ma finished speaking. Biddy's happiness meant too much to him for even a moment of her sadness to go unnoticed.

Finbarr's attempts at music had stopped by the time Ian stepped through the bedroom doorway. Biddy knelt beside the little trundle bed, her back to Ian. Finbarr listened intently as she spoke.

"You may not yet be as fine a musician as you'd like, but that doesn't mean you should stop trying."

The boy's nose scrunched. "I sound terrible."

"Did you know my father played the penny whistle?"

Finbarr perked up. Ian listened more closely as well. Twice in one evening she was speaking of her father.

"I don't remember much about him," she continued, "but I do remember standing outside his house with my mother sometimes, and we could hear him playing inside. The windows didn't have glass so the sound carried. She said his music was how she knew he was in there, thinking of her."

Her da played from inside and never came out, knowing his wife and child were outside listening?

"Wouldn't you enjoy playing for a lass someday?" Biddy asked Finbarr. "'Tis a fine way to tell her you care."

Something in the suggestion made Finbarr uneasy. He shook his head and fidgeted a bit. "Couldn't I just dance with her? I'm a good dancer."

"Dancing does wonders for a lass's opinion of a lad," Biddy said.

Ian leaned against the doorframe. "Does it, now?"

Biddy twisted a bit and looked at him. To his utter relief, she didn't look upset or sad. Her sudden departure had left him with every expectation of seeing both emotions on her face.

Ian shifted his gaze to the lad. "Supper is waiting for you on the table, you scamp." He shooed his brother out. He then helped Biddy to her feet. "You looked upset before. I came to make certain you're well."

She waved off the concern. "I was a bit melancholy, yes, but I only shed a tear or two."

"*Only* doesn't apply to your tears, Biddy Dillon. If you're unhappy, there's no *only* about it."

Her shoulders rose and fell with a shaky breath. "Thinking of my parents is always difficult. There is simply too much left unanswered."

He motioned for her to sit on the edge of the bed then sat beside her. "I know you don't speak of them often, but maybe it'd help if you did."

"A great deal of pain lies along that path, Ian."

He took cautious hold of her good hand. The door was open, eliminating any impropriety. He felt uneasy, not because of the privacy of their situation, but because of the thinness of the ice he'd been treading upon with her the past several days.

"I think I've shown myself a good listener, have I not?"

She met his gaze. "You have."

"And I've not given you reason to think me untrustworthy?"

"No reason at all."

He set his other hand atop his first, sandwiching her hand between his two. "Unburden your mind a bit. It'll do you good, I'm certain of it."

She dropped her gaze to their hands. Neither he nor she spoke or moved. They hardly breathed.

When she did break the silence between them, it was with a whisper. "They left each other."

Ian knew better than to press for more. He did as he'd promised—he simply listened.

"When I was small, not long before we sailed from Ireland, my father went to live in his house, the tall one I spoke of before. I think it was his family's home." She took a fortifying breath and continued with a posture of determination. "Mother and I visited every day, watching for him, waiting for him to come out to us." She swallowed so thickly that he heard it. "He never came out. He never even glanced out the windows. He'd forgotten us, I suppose, or simply didn't care any longer."

Had they ever attempted to go in? Biddy had been very young; she likely didn't remember all the details.

She pulled her hand from his, then stood and paced. "I think he might have come 'round in time, but Mother grew weary of waiting. So she left—not just the grounds, but the country. She and I came to America and left him behind." Her circuits of the tiny room quickened. "For the rest of her life, she insisted that he'd promised to come too. He never did."

He recalled Biddy speaking of families abandoning each other. This, it seemed, was the reason his family's acceptance of her mattered so much, and the reason being alone weighed on her. But which of her parents had truly abandoned the other? Even Biddy didn't seem certain where the blame lay.

"My mother is dead now. I haven't any idea where my father is. I don't speak of them often. Not because I don't care or don't miss them. I simply know how the story ends: with me all alone, wondering if they ever loved each other, or me."

Ian stood and placed himself directly before her. "I wish I knew the answers so you needn't keep asking them of yourself."

"I wish you did, as well." Such sadness filled those blue eyes. "Deep inside I know I'll likely never fully know what happened between them."

"And that is mighty unfair."

She offered a tremulous smile. "It does help to have spoken of it, though. I feel a little less alone in my worries. In these worries, at least."

If only she would allow him to help her bear all her troubles—her fears and uncertainties. He never wanted her to be alone, and he never wanted to be without her.

Chapter Eleven

The family gathered the next Sunday, but the tone was one of anxious anticipation rather than the usual laughter and lightheartedness. Da had something to tell them all. Though he hadn't revealed the subject matter, everyone felt certain they knew: the "opportunity" he'd been offered.

Every eye in the room was on Da. Every eye, that is, except Finbarr's. The little one hadn't moved from the window since returning home from church. He was watching for Biddy. Maura's sister worked for a fine family who, rumor had it, were looking to hire more household help. Biddy was exploring the possibility.

Finbarr missed her. Ian did as well. Desperately.

"I had the chance yesterday to speak with Mr. Grandford's associate, the one whose offering this 'opportunity.' He owns a large valley in the West," Da said from his chair near the fire. "Water is scarcer there than it is here—certainly scarcer than in Ireland. His valley has a good-sized river running through it, but for the land to be farmable, that water has to reach more areas than it does now. He's looking for able bodies to dig canals that can bring the water where it needs to go. He's further hoping to erect buildings and corrals, and widen cart paths into roads, and to build bridges over the river."

Ian was fully capable of digging—hard but mindless work. He was far more intrigued at the possibility of building things. He liked working with his hands.

"In exchange," Da continued, "he means to pay those who come to work for him by giving them land."

The room went utterly silent. The rumor was true, then. They could once again have land of their own.

"We'd need to work for a lot of years before we'd earn enough land for all of us to have our own farms," Da said. "But in the meantime, we'd have enough land to build a large home, with the expanse of a valley around us, plus clean air and dirt beneath our feet."

"How many families are being given this chance?" Tavish thrived on company and friendships. He'd not relish a life of isolation.

"Four or five," Da said. "That number will grow if the land responds well to the work."

"It could become a regular town," Tavish said.

"Perhaps, but only if the man means to split the valley up that much." Da smiled a little. Indeed, he'd not truly stopped smiling from the moment he'd begun sharing the details of the situation. "There's land enough for ranches and distant farms. Any number of other land owners and more towns could lie beyond the borders of his holdings. The area would likely never be crowded, though it won't be empty, either. And unlike most of the West, this corner has water."

"Sounds perfect," Ma said.

Ian watched his family for their reactions. Everyone looked intrigued, though Patrick's expression spoke less of eagerness than of disquiet. Ian's stomach tied in a knot of apprehension at the sight of his brother's uncertainty. Patrick was fond of New York and felt strongly about taking a stand on the crisis that had been unfolding ever since the election of Mr. Lincoln. Did Patrick's passions run deep enough for him to remain here while the rest of the family travelled to a distant valley?

"It won't be like Ireland," Da said in a voice of apologetic warning. "The man says the area is dry and not terribly green. But he says the mountains are majestic. Tall trees grow around the riverbed, and the sky is vast and blue."

Ian could picture it easily. He'd be helping to shape a new area of the country—to work the land, explore the mountains Da'd spoken of. In time, Ian would have his own portion of the valley. He could build his very own house. That image came even clearer in his mind than the valley itself. The house would have a front window facing mountains, a back door opening to his fields.

And Biddy would be there beside him. His Biddy. In *their* home.

"If we decide to take this chance," Da said, "we'll leave at the end of winter, arriving early in the spring."

"The journey will take that long?" Patrick asked.

Da nodded. "'Tis a far spell from the last train station. We'll cover a great deal of the distance by wagon, with only the barest of trails leading in the general direction we're going. For that and many other reasons, this isn't a decision to be made lightly. Once we're there, we're there to stay."

Patrick's mouth turned down. His brow creased sharply. Ma's enthusiasm, however, didn't waver. Ciara and Tavish peppered Da with questions. Ian couldn't hear what Mary and Thomas spoke of between them, but they appeared interested— excited, even. Finbarr still hadn't left the window.

Grady caught Ian's gaze and gave him a questioning look, one that pulled Ian from his chair and tugged him across the room.

"You seem keen on this opportunity," Grady said. "You always did feel a connection to the land. Even when you were a tiny lad, you were happiest working the earth alongside Da."

Those had been grand times for Ian. He still thought back on them regularly. "I'd love to have land again, to be free of the factory and the endless rows of buildings and paved streets."

"Aye," Grady sighed. "New York isn't *alive* in the way we were accustomed to, is it?"

Ian shook his head, dropping into the chair beside Grady's, which was empty after Maura rose to walk about and soothe their fussy baby. "What of the two of you?" Ian asked, nodding to Maura. "Do you mean to come as well?"

"Maura's family all lives here. I don't know that she could bear to be away from them. It'd break her heart, it would."

"And what of your heart, brother?"

"She *is* my heart." Grady's gaze settled on Maura, and his expression turned to one of gentle adoration. "Where she's happy, I'm happy. So where she is, I'll always be."

The words etched themselves into Ian's mind with equal parts conviction and concern. *Where she's happy, I'm happy. So where she is, I'll always be.*

In all Ian's imaginings of a distant promised land in the West, Biddy had been there with him. But what assurance did he have that she would want to go with him? Their courtship, if one could call it that, was only a few short weeks old. He'd not yet managed to tell her he loved her. Indeed, she'd grown more distant of late though his feelings for her had not changed.

"I know that look," Grady said. "You're fretting over a woman."

Ian filled his cheeks with air and pushed it out slowly, trying to release some of his tension with it. "I want to go West."

"I know." Grady watched him intently, clearly sensing there was more.

"But going would mean leaving Biddy behind."

Grady leaned back in his chair. "You don't believe she'd come with you?"

"I've known her only a few weeks. I'd not expect her to take such a risk on a man who's little more than a stranger."

His brother's gaze narrowed on him in a look of contemplation. "Would you go without her?"

The thought immediately twisted into knots inside him. Going without Biddy meant never seeing her again. It meant a life without her. It meant . . . misery. And yet, he didn't know if she cared for him enough to even suggest she come West with him.

"I don't know what to do," he said quietly.

"You don't have to know right this moment. She'll be back before nightfall."

Ian laughed humorlessly. "What is it I'm supposed to say to her when she arrives? 'Good evening to you, Biddy. Will you cross the country with me?'"

Grady shook his head. "I'd suggest, 'Good evening to you, Biddy. How was your day?' You listen to her answer. You talk with her about life and happiness and dreams. Then you do the same thing tomorrow, and the day after that. In time, you'll know if she'd be willing to cross the country with you, and you'll know what you'd do if she isn't."

If she isn't. Saints, he hoped he didn't have to sort out that particular dilemma. And Grady was speaking of time as if they had a great deal of it. That was not at all the case.

"Da needs to give the man a decision," Ian said. "And tell him how many of us there'd be going. And he needs to do it in only a few days."

"Fortunately you have something of a head start on the talking and listening. 'Tis near about all you two've done, from what I hear." Grady leaned closer and lowered his voice. "Maybe you ought to think about kissing the lass."

"I've *thought* about it plenty."

"I imagine you have." Grady stood. "Now, if you'll excuse me, my little one's fussing yet, and his ma looks near to tears."

He crossed to Maura rocking the unhappy little one. Grady

pressed a kiss to his wife's cheek before relieving her of her sobbing burden.

Theirs was the kind of affectionate connection Ian had always wanted to find for himself. Mary and Thomas were much the same way, as were Ma and Da. Only recently had that dream, that hope, become undeniably specific. But did he factor into Biddy's hopes and dreams?

Time would tell, the old saying went. But time was precisely what he was running out of.

Biddy slowed her pace as she approached the O'Connors' tenement building. She'd hoped to return having secured a job and an income so she needn't be a burden on them any longer. Though she would have enjoyed being part of the family's weekly Sunday gathering, she'd delayed her return, making the journey back more slowly than necessary. Mr. O'Connor meant to share with his family the details of the opportunity waiting for them in the West, and she did not want to be there when he did.

The O'Connors had all been so excited at the possibility, so eagerly awaiting every bit of information he offered. She knew in her heart that if the details proved at all promising the family meant to go. She would be left behind. And she hadn't wanted to be there watching them plan their futures without her.

Pull yourself together, Biddy. You cannot fall to pieces over this. People leave. That is simply the way of things.

They would be celebrating a much-deserved bit of good fortune. Far be it from her to dampen their excitement. They'd been good enough to help her, to see her through difficulties. She'd not repay that with misery.

Ciara answered her knock, motioning her inside. The room was crowded. Most everyone was standing, a few moving about. Finbarr rushed over and threw his arms around Biddy, saying how very much he'd missed her and describing the silly game he and Ian had played once again on their way home from church.

Ian. Her heart ached at the sound of that name. In that moment, she needed his strength. She needed his calm presence and the reassurance she always felt when she was with him. He must have been in the room, but she hadn't managed to spot him yet.

Finbarr was still prattling on. The moment he stopped for breath, Biddy spoke. "Where is Ian?" Her voice hardly rose above a whisper. Until she heard the shaky quality of her simple question, she didn't realize how done-in she truly was by recent events.

Finbarr took her by the hand and led her farther into the room, weaving around the crowd. A few steps and a bit of maneuvering found herself standing before the very person she'd most longed to see.

"Biddy asked where you were," Finbarr told his brother. "And she looked sad. So I brought her to you."

Ian turned his kind eyes on her, every inch of his expression filled with empathy. "Are you sad, Biddy?"

She tried to maintain her composure and answer evenly, but she felt herself crumbling. "I've had a difficult day."

And you are going to leave me.

He wrapped his arms around her, careful as always of her still-healing arm, and held her tenderly. She leaned into his embrace, focusing on that moment, on the warmth of him, knowing that all too soon he would be gone and she would never be held this way by him again.

"Were you not given the job, then?" he asked.

"The housekeeper didn't feel I was strong enough."

"I'm sorry."

She leaned more heavily against him. The rest of the family were thoroughly occupied with their own conversations and the meal preparations. They likely didn't notice the tender scene playing out in the back corner of the room. Even if they did, Biddy needed Ian's reassuring tenderness too much in that moment to pull away.

He rubbed her back in slow, calming circles. She found she could breathe deeply again. Even not knowing the entirety of her troubled thoughts, he'd managed to soothe her.

What will I do without him?

"There'll likely be another household hiring when your arm's fully healed," he said. "Ma might know of a place in need of cleaning."

Though she needed to find work, it wasn't the heaviest weight on her heart. She stepped back a bit, looking up into his face rather than leaning her head against his shoulder. His presence bolstered her strength, but knowing the topic the family had discussed before her arrival, she knew she needed to learn to stand on her own. "Did your father have more information about this chance out West?"

"He did indeed." Excitement lit Ian's face on the instant. "We're to be paid in land—actual land—for the keeping. We'll own it rather than being tenants as we were in Ireland. It is a dream come true."

He spoke in decided absolutes. Ian O'Connor had made his decision; he'd chosen his future.

Please give me reason to believe I can be part of that future. Please.

He met her gaze once more. Did he mean to tell her his thoughts and feelings? Did he mean to give her the hope she so desperately needed?

"We've set aside a bit of supper for you," Ian said. "That may help lift your spirits a little."

Supper? *That* was all the more he meant to speak to her about? Did he not mean to say anything more personal than that?

Give me reason to hope.

He didn't say a word.

"I'm not very hungry just now," she said. "I'm too weary to eat."

"You should lie down. Resting will do you a world of good, I'm sure of it." Ian turned away, motioning to his mother to come over, then quickly making arrangements with her for Biddy to rest in the bedroom, away from the noise. Away from the family.

Away from him.

She lay there in the dim room, alone, for what felt like hours, listening to the O'Connors' voices raised in jovial conversation. They sounded so eager and enthusiastic about their new future. Life was looking up for the O'Connors.

She swiped at an escaping tear. "We make the best of it," she whispered. "Come what may, we make the best of it."

Chapter Twelve

"You're a coward, Ian O'Connor." Patrick's quiet declaration told Ian that he wasn't the only one still awake in the flat, though night had long since fallen.

Ian sat on his rumpled blankets. He kept his gaze on the back wall, not so much as glancing at his brother. His mind was heavy enough without the added condemnation.

"You had her in your arms. Upon returning, she sought you out first thing. She *reached* for you. If ever a man was handed the answers to where a woman's heart lay, it was you in that moment. And what did you do? Did you tell her you cared for her? That you wanted her to come with you out West? Did you say your heart would never be whole without her?"

"I haven't your gift for fine speeches," Ian muttered.

"You might have made an awkward speech then. Bumbled your way through it. Anything other than telling the poor lass that she looked tired and ought to lie down."

"How is it, Patrick, that at seventeen, you're such an expert?"

"I have three older brothers, one of whom I've spent every day of my life with. That's how. I've learned a thing or two."

Ian shook his head. "Considering *I* am that brother, your logic doesn't hold up."

"You think you've taught me nothing?" Patrick sat up as well. His tone turned uncharacteristically serious. "You're my older brother, the member of the family from whom I've learned the most. You're—you're my best friend, Ian." In a tone of jesting, he added, "Even if you are a dunce with the lasses."

Ian groaned. "Grady told me to just kiss her."

Patrick made a sound of clear approval. "That could've worked, provided you aren't terrible at it."

Ian dropped his head against the wall behind them. "I . . . couldn't."

"Couldn't what? Kiss her?"

"Tell her how I'm feeling, what I hope for." He very nearly had told her, though. The confession had hovered on his lips only to be silenced by his own doubts and uncertainty. "What if she doesn't feel the same?"

Patrick moved to face him directly. "What if she does?"

Ian tipped his chin up, his gaze lifting to the darkened ceiling. "How could she? I have so little to offer. I can't imagine—"

"It's a risk," Patrick said. "I'll not deny that. But if you care about her—"

"I *love* her."

"Exactly," Patrick said. "Doesn't that make her worth the gamble?"

The truth of his brother's words penetrated Ian's uncertain mind with unexpected force. "For a little brother, you're very wise."

"And for an older brother, you're not half bad." The declaration was equal parts jesting and earnest.

Ian stood and squared his shoulders. He'd make his confession to Biddy and hope for the best. He pushed back the hanging quilt.

"She'll be asleep," Patrick warned.

But she wasn't. Ian spotted her at the very window where Finbarr had stationed himself all that Sunday, watching for her return. She'd wrapped herself in a quilt, her hair hanging in waves around her shoulders. Ian saw her only in profile, but her hunched posture and hanging head told him her spirits were low. He knew the feeling well.

"Take the risk," Patrick whispered.

Take the risk.

He let the quilt fall into place behind him. His stockinged feet hardly made a sound as he carefully crossed the room. He passed the quilt behind which Tavish slept. Ciara was asleep on the floor near the fireplace. Finbarr's trundle bed had been rolled out to its usual spot not far from the bed Biddy ought to have been resting on. Navigating the narrow bits of open floor took effort. Ian didn't dare risk waking anyone by crashing into furniture or people.

"Why are you still awake?" Biddy asked as he approached.

He followed Biddy's lead and kept his voice low. "I've a heavy mind just now."

Biddy took a shaky breath then turned to face him. "I've something to say, Ian, and I mean to say it while I've courage enough."

That sounded familiar.

She pressed on. "I've nothing and no one in this city. No reason for staying."

She had no one? Surely she didn't include him in that declaration.

"You know your family better than I do," she continued. "If I offered to work for them, to help earn the land they're hoping for, do you think they would allow me to go West with them?"

She wanted to come West.

With the family, he silently amended. 'Twasn't the declaration of undying love he'd've preferred, but it was encouraging.

"I would be no trouble." Biddy's voice took on an almost frantic earnestness. "I'll work hard and won't require any space other than a corner of the floor. I can cook and do the wash, so I'd be an asset to the household." Her pleading eyes locked with his. "Would you ask them for me? I think they'd be more willing to consider it if you made the request."

This was what she wanted from him? "I'll not ask my parents to take you on as a servant, Biddy."

"They wouldn't have to pay me." She clutched his arm with her good hand, her injured arm hanging limply at her side. The look in her eyes was utterly frantic.

Had he done such a poor job of his short-lived courtship that she thought unpaid servitude was her only welcome among them?

106

"Would you be happy living that way?" he asked.

"I—" Her posture slumped further. "I wouldn't be alone. And I wouldn't be left behind."

Left behind. She'd seen her parents leave the other. Living with uncertainty had plagued her for too long.

He determined to offer what reassurance he could. "I've thought about what you told me of your parents, and I think maybe you've misunderstood a few things."

Moonlight illuminated her wary expression.

"Sit with me a moment," he said.

She didn't object. They moved carefully around Finbarr's sleeping form, then Ciara's. When they were comfortably situated near the fireplace, she turned to him, watching and waiting in silence.

"If my cyphering is correct, you left Ireland in '47."

She nodded, the movement barely visible in the dim light of the embers.

"And you were in County Mayo, where the Hunger raged hard and fierce in its early years. So fierce, in fact, that many a poor Irishman, desperate to save his family from starvation, stole the food they needed. Far too many endured steep sentences for their . . . crimes."

She didn't answer, and he couldn't see her well enough to guess at her silent reaction. He hadn't intended to discuss the topic, but the unknowns about her past weighed on her. He couldn't bear to see her suffer.

"You spoke of a large building with rows of windows far above your head with bars in the frames but no glass. You and your mother visited often but never went inside, and your father never came out." He could so easily picture a building like the one she'd described. "I'd wager no one ever came out."

"Not that I recall," she said.

"I have an uncle who spent a very long time in a building with rows of glassless windows and imposing walls. No one ever came in or out of it either. No one was permitted to."

"Oh, heavens," she whispered.

"I've my suspicions the place you remember wasn't an oversized house at all."

He could see by the shaking of her hands that she was following his thought on the matter. "You think it might have been a prison."

"I can't know for sure, but it makes sense." He held her hand, hoping to offer comfort. "My uncle lived in an area severely stricken by the Hunger. When he couldn't bear the sight of starving children any longer, he took to stealing food to keep them alive. He was caught and imprisoned. Ireland's jails were full to bursting during those agonizing years with people guilty of the great crime of being poor and hungry. Your father might very well have been among that number."

She rocked back and forth, the movement as tense as it was tiny. 'Twas a difficult thing rearranging one's view of the past.

"You and your mother were likely starving and couldn't stay until his sentence was complete. Your mother 'left him' to save your lives."

She took a quavering breath. "But he never came, not in twelve years."

Ian took her hand. "Fate was not always kind to those prisoners, dear. The ones who weren't transported often finished their time in prison weak and ill. When they were released, they got thrust into a land that would continue to be ravaged by famine for years—for a long time after you and your mother sought safety over the seas."

She gazed straight ahead at the glowing embers in the fireplace. "Do you think that is what happened to him? To my parents?"

"It is a possibility."

She rose, tension filling her movements. She tucked her quilt more snuggly about herself. A long moment passed before she spoke. "They might not have abandoned each other after all. They didn't simply give up on each other and leave."

"No, I don't think they did, dear."

She returned to the window, gazing out once more. "People leave; they walk away. That was the first truth I ever learned. I have lived all my life with the fear of people abandoning me."

Did she think he meant to do just the same to her? Simply walk away?

Take the risk. Say what needs saying.

He rose and moved closer, though not all the way to her side. "We've not known each other long, and I'll not pretend there's been time enough or closeness enough for a deep and abiding connection to have grown between us."

She didn't look back, didn't move.

"I want you to go West," he said. "I've wanted it from the first moment Da told us of the possibility. But I didn't know how to ask. I wasn't certain you'd want to come with—" He almost said *us* but knew that choice for the coward's path it was. If he was to deserve her affection in any way, he needed to be strong enough—brave enough—to take this leap. "I want you to come with *me*."

"With you?"

He heard the whispered question only because she had at last turned to face him. "I haven't a talent for words and speeches," he said, feeling that lack terribly at the moment.

"I don't need fine speeches."

"How do you feel about terribly muddled ones?" That seemed the likeliest outcome.

Biddy pushed out a loud, frustrated breath. "Do not torture me, Ian O'Connor. And do not make light of this. I've carried these worries all my life. Years of uncertainty are bubbling over just now."

Ian ran his hands down her arm. A tear-clogged whimper escaped her. For the length of a breath, he thought he'd taken hold of her injured arm rather than her whole one. But the truth of the situation sorted itself. Hers was pain of the heart, not the body. He pulled her into his embrace, and she held tightly to him.

"Oh, Ian," she whispered in broken tones.

"My darling, Biddy. Leaving you is not a possibility. Not now. Not ever." He held her close, mindful of her injuries. "If you tell me right now that you'd rather not go West, that you mean to stay in New York, then I will stay as well, willingly and happily, with no regrets."

SARAH M. EDEN

"But your land. It's your dream."

He turned his head enough to press a kiss to her temple. "*You* are my dream, Biddy, and my dearest love."

She turned a little in his arms, looking up into his face. "You love me?"

"With all my heart." He brushed his lips against her forehead. "I know it's a large jump to take so soon, but I want to spend my life with you. I want to be with you always and forever."

The glint of moonlight on her face illuminated the first hints of a smile. "I would like that."

He stumbled a bit over his response. "You would?"

He could only just make out the first hints of a blush on her face. "I love you, Ian. I have for weeks now."

His heart leapt into his throat. She loved him. His angel, his Biddy, loved him. "Enough to cross a continent with me?"

"I'd go anywhere in all this world with you. You need only ask."

He took her hand in his, lifting it to his lips and tenderly kissing her fingers. "Will you build a new life with me?"

She raised up on her toes, her quilt sliding to the floor around their feet. "Of course, my love."

She kissed his cheek, lingering there for a long moment. An unexpected wish seized him in the moment, one he found himself unable to resist. He snaked an arm around her waist and with his free hand, took hold of hers. "Dance with me?"

"Are you taking Finbarr's advice now?"

The lad had recommended dancing as a means of courting.

Ian leaned his forehead against hers. "My brothers have grand ideas now and then."

He lightly swayed them back and forth, not a true dance, there not being room enough, his heart pounding just the same.

"This was good advice," Biddy said. "Are any of the others as wise as Finbarr?"

"Patrick said to tell you how I feel."

She nodded. "And you did."

"I did. And Grady had a bit of advice as well."

Biddy met his eye. "What did he suggest?"

At that, the pounding in his chest became a battering. "He said . . . I ought to kiss you."

Far from being shocked or turning bashful, Biddy held his gaze. "He's right, you know."

"I do know." Ian slipped his hand from hers and cupped her cheek.

A slow, warm smile formed on her beloved face. He would never grow tired of seeing her happy nor feeling her in his arms.

"I believe Tavish's advice would be to stop draggin' your feet, Ian."

He closed the final inches between them. She hooked her arm around his neck. He wrapped both his arms around her middle. After one small breath—a brief pause to cherish the moment—Ian bent and placed a whisper of a kiss on her lips. Anticipation tiptoed over him as he kissed her again, more fully, more deeply. She held to him, returning his attentions with tender passion.

How long he kissed her, he couldn't say. It felt like lifetimes, yet passed in the length of a breath. For long moments afterward, he returned to the pleasure of simply holding her in his arms, the moonlight spilling through the windows.

"I was certain when I first saw you that you were an angel. But I never imagined you would be *my* heaven-sent miracle."

She sighed, her head resting once more on his shoulder. "And you, Ian O'Connor, are mine."

Chapter Thirteen

In the morning, Biddy rose when the first of the family did. As always, they were careful not to wake those whose days began and ended later. Ian, however, looked ready to burst. The night before, she and Ian had decided to tell his parents of their engagement over breakfast while the rest of the family still slept. Patrick, if the grins he tossed her were any indication, already knew.

The brothers had a deep and unique connection. Anyone who spent even a moment with them could see as much. They laughed together often, but also shared moments that were personal and solemn. More than once, Biddy had caught them exchanging looks of understanding over some unspoken shared experience. Ian's bond with all his family was strong, but Patrick claimed a place in his heart that was fiercely important and essential. Seeing the depth of that attachment gave her further faith in the future she and Ian would build together. Ian's was a loyal and loving heart, and she had a claim on that devotion.

Patrick joined her at the fireplace, where she stirred the pot of porridge. Ciara was still sleeping nearby, so they spoke low and moved quietly.

"I'm to have another sister, am I?" His tone gave every indication of approval.

"He told you."

Patrick smiled. "He didn't have to."

"You aren't disappointed in his choice?" 'Twas her greatest concern over the coming announcement. What if she was wrong, and the O'Connors didn't want her in their family?

"He's never been a truly *un*happy person, but since you arrived in his life, he's happier than I've ever seen him. His face lights whenever you're near. The lines of worry on his face ease when he speaks of you."

"He speaks of me?"

Patrick laughed, but quickly cut himself off with a worried look at his sleeping sister. She didn't stir. He continued, his voice subdued once more. "Of course he does. He speaks of little else, in fact."

She covered her embarrassment with a jesting reply. "That must be a bit monotonous for you."

"'Tis the reason I'm glad he's marrying you at last. I'll not have to listen to him anymore." His expression turned solemn. "I'll miss having him here every day, miss talking with him all the time. If I'd the least doubt you were the very best person in the world for my brother, I don't think I'd be willing to part with him."

"I don't imagine we'll be so far away as all that." The other married O'Connor siblings all lived quite nearby.

He nodded, but didn't speak further.

Ian arrived at her side in the very next moment. "Patrick, will you see to the porridge? Biddy and I mean to talk with Da and Ma."

Patrick wiggled his eyebrows, earning him a lighthearted shoulder shove from his brother.

"Don't wake your sister," Biddy warned.

Her future brother-in-law actually rolled his eyes. "I see whose side you mean to take in this family."

"Ian's," she answered firmly.

"Go share your news." Patrick took the spoon from her. "Then the shouts of joy can be blamed if Ciara doesn't stay asleep."

Ian slipped his arm around Biddy's waist and turned her toward the table. "How is your arm this morning? You seem to be favoring it more than usual."

"It isn't terrible," she said.

"That is not very reassuring."

She leaned her head against his shoulder as they took the few steps required to cross the small room. The years had taught her to face her troubles alone. Her heart warmed knowing that she no longer had to. In time she might no longer need to continually remind herself that she was not on her own anymore.

Ma sat at the table, something she didn't often do during morning meal preparations. "I don't know how you convinced that brother of yours to take over the cooking, but I wholeheartedly approve."

Ian held a chair for Biddy, which she took without comment. Nervousness had seized her mind, making words impossible. He sat beside her then took her hand. "We've something to tell you," he said to his parents.

"Have you?" Why did Mr. O'Connor look on the verge of laughing?

An amused light twinkled in Mrs. O'Connor's eyes as well. Ian looked from one parent to the other, suspicion narrowing his gaze.

"You've sorted it, have you?" he said.

"You haven't exactly made it difficult, son," Mr. O'Connor said. "The only question any of us have in our minds is how long you intend to wait."

Had they truly guessed at the state of things? Biddy watched them closely, bracing herself against any signs of disapproval. She saw only smiles, only kindness and happiness.

"We'll need to find a place of our own," Ian said. "And Biddy'll need to heal enough to find work. Other than that, we've no reason to put it off."

Mrs. O'Connor turned to face Biddy more fully. "Men are forever jumping over the best bits of this, intent on addressing the dull parts." She set her hand atop Biddy and Ian's entwined ones. "Has he asked you to marry him, then?"

Mrs. O'Connor was perfectly aware of the answer, of course, yet there was such comfort in being permitted to make the situation entirely clear.

"He has," she said.

Mrs. O'Connor turned a somewhat piercing eye on her son.

"Did you ask the question tenderly, or did you skip straight to discussing housing arrangements and wages?"

Biddy jumped to Ian's defense. "He took his brothers' advice."

"That could be good or bad," Mr. O'Connor muttered.

"It was quite good," Biddy said. "Especially Finbarr's words of wisdom."

"Little Finbarr?" Mrs. O'Connor laughed on the words. "What could he possibly have suggested?"

"Dancing," she said.

Mrs. O'Connor's expression turned unmistakably fond and maternal. "That boy does love music."

Mr. O'Connor folded his hands atop the table. "So Ian proposed, didn't make a mull of it, and you've accepted."

That was the sum of it. "I hope you approve." How difficult speaking those four words proved to be for Biddy. She needed to know if she'd be accepted, yet feared the answer.

"Oh, dear girl," Mr. O'Connor said, "we couldn't be happier."

Ian leaned closer to her and whispered, "Neither could I."

She rested against him, a lifetime of anxiety, rejections, and abandonment easing in that moment. In time, she might stop fearing such things entirely, but old worries didn't resolve themselves in an instant.

Patrick joined them, setting steaming bowls of porridge on the table. He barely held back a smirk. Eying his parents, he asked, "Have you recovered from the shock of their announcement?"

"Only just." Mr. O'Connor met the jest with one of his own before swiftly returning to more practical topics. "We'll talk with Father Braden on Sunday and make arrangements. In the meantime, keep your ear to the ground. We'll find Biddy a position and the two of you a flat nearby to tide you over until spring."

Spring. When they would all be going West. Only the day before, Biddy had been terrified at the thought of being left behind. She'd resigned herself to the hope of traveling as the family's servant, if need be. Instead, she would be going as one of them. She would be with Ian, building a new life. Together.

Patrick bent over his bowl of porridge, suddenly very quiet. Ian eyed his brother and grew quiet as well. Mr. and Mrs. O'Connor took up a conversation regarding when to make their springtime journey and what arrangements would be necessary.

Biddy, tucked up close to Ian, lowered her voice to a whisper. "Is something the matter with Patrick? He's so quiet of a sudden."

"He's not decided if he means to go West with us," Ian answered almost silently, pain evident in his features.

"He would stay behind?" She'd never have imagined such a thing. This family was so connected, so close. To leave any member behind was unthinkable.

Ian nodded. "Grady as well. His wife's family is all here."

"This 'opportunity' means splitting your family."

He held her closer, as if having her there eased some of his worry and sorrow. "I'm holding out hope that Patrick will choose to come."

"And if he doesn't?"

He took a breath, long and audible and tense. His gaze fell on Patrick, who hadn't looked up from his meal. Ian said nothing; Biddy suspected he couldn't.

She turned enough in her chair to face him more fully. His eyes met hers. "Come what may," she said, "we'll make the best of it."

She'd repeated her mother's words again and again over the years, but never had they brought such a feeling of comfort. No longer did they feel like a declaration borne of survival, but a promise of hope.

Ian pressed a light kiss to her forehead. "And we'll make the best of it together."

"Together," she repeated in an amazed whisper.

She who had been on her own for so long, need never be alone again.

Chapter Fourteen

MARCH 1861

Spring arrived and, with it, departure day. The O'Connors—most of them, at least—were leaving yet another home in search of yet another promised land.

"What'll we do for furniture?" Ciara eyed the sparse assortment of belongings that would be making the journey with them.

"We'll make do," Da said. Ma handed him her carpet bag, and he set it beside the family's lone traveling trunk in Grady's wagon.

The matter of furniture had been settled weeks ago. Quite simply, they hadn't the means of transporting any across a country, which would have required higher train fare and more wagons once they reached the end of the line. They'd simply have to find a means of replacing what they'd not been able to bring.

"Don't you worry, Ciara," Grady said. "Maura and I will take good care of all you're leaving behind."

"I wish you were coming with us." Ciara spoke the regret they all felt.

"The man who owns the land has sent Da letters, and we can do the same. We'll hear from each other, you'll see." Grady gave Ciara a firm, brotherly hug.

Biddy stepped up beside Ian, slipping her hand in his. Months had passed since the day her arm had been mangled. Ian still thanked the heavens regularly that she'd healed so entirely. He'd offered daily prayers of gratitude for the miracle she was in his life. They'd been married a little over four months, and he still found himself shocked at his good fortune.

She stood with her hand in his, eying their gathered family. A cool spring breeze pulled wisps of her hair loose. "This will be a difficult goodbye for everyone."

"Aye." He pushed back a sigh. "We'll have so much distance between us and so much uncertainty."

Only a couple of weeks earlier, the recently seceded states had formed their own government, seizing forts and other federal properties. Attempts at compromise and dampening the flames of conflict had failed one after another. War seemed unavoidable now. 'Twas one of the reasons Da wished to make an earlier start of their journey than they'd originally planned. The looming war was by far the biggest reason Ian worried about Patrick staying.

"I believe in this country," he had said the night he'd told them all he wouldn't be leaving New York. "I believe in what it's meant to stand for. Some things"—he echoed his own advice to Ian only a few months earlier—"are worth the risk."

Though they'd neither of them told Ma, Patrick had confided that, should the war they all anticipated break out, he intended to join the Irish Brigade out of New York and fight for the future of the Union. Ian was proud of his brother's strength of conviction, but he feared for him. War was no small thing.

A light kiss on his cheek pulled him from his heavy thoughts. Biddy gave him an empathetic look.

He tucked her into his embrace. "Are you ready for this adventure, my love? This new life may very well be the hardest thing we'll ever undertake."

"Or it may be the most wonderful." Few things warmed his heart as fully as the sight of his Biddy—his bride—smiling joyously.

"Let us aim for that, then. This new life will be wonderful."

Tavish walked past them with a theatrical roll of his eyes. "Are we going to have to listen to sweet talk all the way West?"

"Someday, brother, you'll find yourself a sweet and fiery colleen who'll steal your heart, and I will enjoy plaguing you with all the things you've been saying to me."

Tavish just laughed and climbed into the wagon bed.

"I need to check one more time," Ma said and slipped inside again. Da and Grady looked over the bags and trunk.

"It's nearly time," Biddy said, squeezing Ian's fingers.

"That it is."

"Ian, love." Biddy rubbed his arm with her free hand. "You need to bid Patrick farewell."

Ian had been avoiding his brother all morning. The moment could not be put off forever, but he dreaded it. Ian had few memories of life before Patrick's birth. In the nearly eighteen years since, he'd not gone a single day without Patrick's company. They'd seen each other through the rough and difficult sea voyage from Ireland. They'd taken jobs beside each other and occupied their small corner of the flat these past eight years.

Despite the difference in their age and personality, they were the very best of friends. As close as two brothers could be. Leaving without Patrick would feel like leaving behind a piece of himself.

"I don't know that I can," he whispered.

"You can." Biddy had been a source of strength to him again and again these past months. "You'll hold out hope, as my mother did, that fate will see you reunited again. And you, my darling Ian, will be proven right in that. You'll see."

They'd told Da and Ma about Ian's suspicions regarding Biddy's father, as their memories of those times were more precise than his. Both agreed that her father had likely been imprisoned for some desperate act as Ian had guessed, that her parents had not been separated by indifference, malice, or even by choice at all. While their story didn't end happily, Biddy had begun speaking of her parents in tones of tenderness instead of pain, and tones of hope instead of despair. The change warmed Ian's heart. Her strength buoyed his own.

"This is more a temporary separation than a final goodbye," he assured himself. "Time may pass, but we'll see each other again."

"I'm sure of it," she said.

Patrick stood leaning against the side of the building. He watched Ian as he approached, wearing his ever-present grin. "So, you're off to be a farmer, are you?"

"You could come," Ian answered. "We've room enough."

"The only thing I miss about farming, Ian, is working alongside you."

Ian leaned on the wall beside him. "We were quite a team, weren't we?"

"The very best," Patrick said. "But you've a fine partner now. An angel, for sure."

"She is that."

Patrick's expression sobered. "You take good care of that sweet Biddy of yours. She's good for you, more than you realize, I think. You be good for her."

Biddy was just then laughing with Mary and Ciara. How quickly she'd found her place among them all. 'Twas as if she'd always been part of their family. More than that, having her in his life felt as natural as breathing, and every bit as essential.

"Grady gave Grandfather O'Connor's watch to Tavish," Patrick said.

That was fitting. "He always has loved that watch."

"And Ma gave Maura the blanket her ma brought with her from Scotland."

"I'm glad you're staying with Grady and Maura," Ian said. "You'll not be alone."

"You'll not be, either."

Ian shoved his hands into his pockets. "I'm grateful to you for your part in that. If not for your encouragement and prodding, I'd not've found the courage to say to her what needed saying."

Patrick smiled. "I think you would've eventually."

"Well, since I'll not be here when you meet a woman who steals your heart away, allow me to return the favor. Say what needs saying. Take the risk. Do what needs doing. Don't be a coward."

Patrick chuckled. "I'll bear that in mind."

"And, Patrick, if the fractures in this nation lead to war—"

He pulled away from the wall, standing at his full height, shoulders squared. "Don't you try talking me out of fighting."

Ian held his hands up in a show of surrender. "I know how strongly you feel about it. I only wanted to say, please be careful. Please . . ." He couldn't find words to express his worry. In the end, all he could do was repeat himself. "Be careful."

Patrick pulled him into a firm, brotherly embrace. "Until we meet again."

"Soon, I hope." Ian lingered a moment longer, unsure what more to say, not yet ready to leave.

Ma came outside once more, Da at her side. Their goodbyes with two of their sons would be tearful and emotional. Ian knew himself unequal to watching that scene unfold. He gave his brother one more heartfelt embrace, then returned to the wagon, where Biddy stood, waiting.

She didn't speak nor ask him to. She simply put her arms around his middle and held tightly to him. He breathed through the pain and the mourning until he could trust himself to speak.

"We'd best be on our way, love. The train waits for no one."

She kept near his side, settling beside him in the back of the wagon. Maura stood on the front steps of the tenement, cradling little Aidan in her arms. Patrick stood beside her. Da and Ma sat up alongside Grady, who was driving them all to the train station before returning to the tiny portion of their family remaining in the city.

Ian kept his eyes on Patrick as the wagon rolled down the road. Biddy tucked herself against him, offering him silent strength and understanding.

The solemn mood followed them down streets wide and narrow as they traveled farther and farther from the place they'd called home, farther from the members of their family they were leaving behind.

Among them all, only Finbarr seemed to have retained his excitement. "Tell me the story again, Da."

The story. 'Twas how Finbarr spoke of this journey—as a story, a mythical adventure. Da always obliged. In that moment, with hearts heavy and an uncertain future ahead of them, a story seemed precisely what they all needed.

"Far away, beyond the very ends of what we know and where we've been, lies a wide valley." Da set his arm around Ma as he spoke. "Though much of the world all around it is dry and sparse, this valley is lush, with a river roaring through it and snowcapped mountains near enough for traveling to."

Ciara turned her tear-filled eyes to Da. Tavish, holding tight to the pocket watch he'd been given, listened intently as well. Thomas set his hand inside Mary's as the words flowed over them all. Ian held fast to Biddy.

"There's land enough for dozens of families," Da continued. "A few have been chosen to come to dig canals and begin the work of planting, to lay down roads and build bridges. This valley, so filled with promise and potential, sits empty and waiting, longing for us to call it home and fill it with our dreams."

Ian kissed Biddy's forehead and held her close. They had so many dreams, dreams they would build together.

"'Tis a magical place, this far-off valley. And that is where we will build our new lives, on the banks of this river, in the midst of this valley, in our very own corner of the world, a bit of paradise known as Hope Springs."

About the Author

SARAH M. EDEN is the *USA Today* bestselling author of multiple historical romances, including Foreword Review's 2013

"IndieFab Book of the Year" gold medal winner for Best Romance, *Longing for Home*, and two-time Whitney Award Winner *Longing for Home: Hope Springs.* Combining her obsession with history and affinity for tender love stories, Sarah loves crafting witty characters and heartfelt romances. She has thrice served as the Master of Ceremonies for the Storymakers Writers Conference and acted as the Writer in Residence at the Northwest Writers Retreat. Sarah is represented by Pam Victorio at D4EO Literary Agency.

Visit Sarah at www.Sarahmeden.com

Photograph © Annalisa Rosenvall